CU00806556

Faint Heart

and other stories

— ◆ —

BIRMINGHAM LIBRARIES

DISCARD

Jack Hopkins

Faint Heart
and other stories

——— ◆ ———

Copyright © 2008 Jack Hopkins

The moral right of the author has been asserted.

Apart from any fair dealing for the purposes of research or private study,
or criticism or review, as permitted under the Copyright, Designs and Patents
Act 1988, this publication may only be reproduced, stored or transmitted, in
any form or by any means, with the prior permission in writing of the
publishers, or in the case of reprographic reproduction in accordance with
the terms of licences issued by the Copyright Licensing Agency. Enquiries
concerning reproduction outside those terms should be sent to the publishers.

Matador
9 De Montfort Mews
Leicester LE1 7FW, UK
Tel: (+44) 116 255 9311 / 9312
Email: books@troubador.co.uk
Web: www.troubador.co.uk/matador

BIRMINGHAM CITY COUNCIL (CBC)	
HJ	11/07/2008
	£6.99
YARDLEY WOOD	

ISBN 978 1906510 121

Typeset in 12pt Times by Troubador Publishing Ltd, Leicester, UK

Matador is an imprint of Troubador Publishing Ltd

This book is dedicated to all those members of writing groups in all parts of the country who meet and hope to create something of lasting value. Those groups that I have belonged to have provided me with the spur to put a finger or two to a keyboard and sometimes achieve a small smile of encouragement. Thank you.

In addition I must mention the Lord Mayor Treloar College where I spent the last happy dozen years of my working life before retirement. To the students, staff, ex-students and ex-staff my best wishes.

Contents

— ◆ —

Faint Heart

— ◆ —

Harry was not a happy hedgehog. It seemed that, every time he wanted to cross the road, a car would snarl towards him and Harry's spines would stand on end as the vicious tyres hissed by his quivering body.

Poor Harry was desperate. Hilda Hedgehog had, on several occasions given him the eye but she always seemed to be on the other side of the road. Harry would try to re-assure himself by repeating the well-known fact that the odds were strongly in favour of a successful crossing without being flattened but though Harry was a hedgehog, he was also a chicken.

Spring came and Harry's thoughts turned to thoughts of Hilda. Meeting a suitable Hedgehog of the opposite sex was not easy at the best of times. Harry could not sleep and when he did, his dreams were all of Hilda.

Harry was desperate.

One fine evening, as the sun was setting behind the corporation rubbish tip Harry sat, moaning to Cyril about his problem.

"It's alright for you," wailed Harry. "You're just a snail and there are snails everywhere and the 'opposite sex' is not a significant factor."

Cyril had just found a crunchy piece of decaying lettuce and was enjoying a late snack. He munched thoughtfully and made an effort to appear sympathetic.

"What you need," he said slowly "Is a really strong super shell, like mine but bigger of course and a lot more stronger."

Harry sniffed, "Don't suppose Hilda would fancy me if I looked like a giant snail."

"Well I've seen humans wearing shells just like mine, on their heads and they don't look stupid. Perhaps we could find you one."

By then it was nearly dark and so they agreed to meet the following morning and, together search for a human head shell.

The next day, progress was slow. Cyril was not renowned for his speed and Harry did not like to move too far ahead or appear impatient. Matters were held up when Cyril met another snail. They appeared to be mutually attracted and Harry withdrew to a discrete distance for some days while Cyril and partner enjoyed the spring hormonal surge. The search was resumed when Cyril returned.

Some weeks later they finally found it, a shiny black crash helmet with red and blue flashes and a clear plastic shield which dropped down to make a windscreen.

Harry spent some time perfecting the art of steering the helmet with his nose from the inside. He realised that, even with all this extra protection, he would need to make the crossing at speed. He practised for many days until he could run fast, inside the helmet, frantically pushing with his nose. He thought that he was ready but, the constant pushing with his nose had made his nose bright red and he had to rest it for a fortnight until it had resumed normality.

Harry picked his crossing point with care. There was a grassy bank on his side where he could pick up speed and he could see, on the other side of the road, a hedge that would help with the braking.

One, late summer evening as the moon glinted on the quiet road, Harry made his crossing. Harry, in his helmet, crashed in to the far hedge and emerged triumphantly, to see that he had also bowled over the lovely Hilda who had been resting in the hedge.

"You're much too late" said Hilda, "I can't stop now. I've got my babies to feed."

Second Chance

— ◆ —

Once upon a time, a young man named Arthur decided that the simple life in Happy Ever Aftia was not for him. He intended to be different. He wanted to be a Somebody and so he went to away to study, to learn a profession. Now, five years later, on the door of his pretty, red tiled roofed cottage, was a brass plaque that announced:

Arthur Grunge
Divorce Lawyer

Each day Arthur polished the plaque and waited. Each day he examined his appointment book and each evening he turned the page to another blank sheet.

Princess Cindy looked out from the topmost castle turret. She could hear the merry village sounds but her spirits stayed low. For one thing, her feet hurt. There were 403 stone steps to climb to reach this peaceful room but she needed the peace, she needed time to think.

The sad Princess looked down at the village below. She could trace all the streets, all the shops. There was the sweetshop that sold such delicious everlasting bulls eyes there, the health and beauty salon run by her stepsisters, Hermione and Petal and there, knitting in her garden, content in her retirement, she could see her Fairy Godmother. As usual, a crowd of villagers, having seen the golden haired princess were cheering and clapping. How they loved their beautiful Princess Cindy! One has to smile and wave back, she thought but her mind kept straying to the little house on which she had seen the plaque which read: "Arthur Grunge, Divorce Lawyer."

The castle drawbridge crashed and two horsemen rode out. Cindy recognised them. It was her husband, Princy with Dandini, his constant companion.

Cindy had a busy afternoon. The Marketing Manager of the "Glass Shoe Co. (By Appt.) was showing the proposed new designs for the "Princess Line."

"Buttons, do you think anyone will want to buy these designs? They all seem so contented wearing clogs."

"Cinders, you just rely on me. I know what I'm doing. As long as you are seen wearing the designs we get all the publicity we need and we make a pile of gold selling clogs with the same designer label."

"If you say so dear Buttons. If you're sure it's legal. One must think of the foot health of all those dear villagers."

"Sure, sure, Princess, just sign here. Ta. I was chatting to your Dad this morning, he says your stepmum's gone to the Magic kingdom for a mid-week break. I think he's pleased to get the break himself."

"Perhaps one should go and visit him. Maybe he's lonely."

"Shouldn't think so Cinders, when I saw him he had all the company he could handle or, should I say, he was handling all the company he could manage. Know what I mean?"

Buttons left, leaving the princess staring gloomily at one's feet.

Cindy retired early to bed that evening and it was not until much later that she was disturbed by the returning Princy.

"I'm sorry old thing, for being so late," he said, kissing her foot peeping below the duvet, "Dandy and I have been having so much fun that I did not realise how late it was."

Cindy pulled back her foot under the duvet and pretended to sleep. That's it! she thought, Tomorrow morning I'm off to see Grunge!

It was never easy for the Princess to leave the castle without the waiting photographers recording the event but she had learnt that, if she stuck to a routine they soon learnt that following her would not produce more pictures than they already had. Cindy tripped across the drawbridge in her figure-hugging tracksuit and trainers, jumped into he mini pumpkin and with a cheery smile to the photographers, zoomed away.

She did not stop at her stepsisters' gym but taking a round about route, arrived outside the lawyer's house. Disguised in dark glasses and a headscarf, she hurried to the door.

Arthur Grunge was feeling disheartened. Two years of blank diary. Two years of no work. Rat Tat what was that! Somebody at the door! For some moments he could not think what to do. This had never happened before. There was somebody at his door!

When Arthur had collected his wits enough to open the door he was surprised to see a slender, track suited lady wearing enormous sunglasses. He recognised her immediately but, panic! should he bow or curtsey? Before his mind could resolve the question she had swept by him into the hall.

"You've got to help me Mr Grunge. I am in desperate trouble."
Tears rolled from beneath her dark glasses.
Grunge struggled to regain his composure.

"Do you have an appointment?" he asked, scanning the pages of his diary.

"No, no, but you've got to help me. Can't you fit me in? I don't mind waiting."

Grunge looked serious. "Hmm, I think I could squeeze you in. Let's just take down a few particulars and we will see what we can do to be of assistance. Your name is?"

"Princess Cindy. I mean, Her Royal Highness The Princess Cinderella of Happy Ever Aftia."

Grunge felt his heart pounding and his palms sweating as he looked at the vision now sitting on the other side of his desk. The first person to ever sit in that chair is Princess Cindy, he thought. This is the big time!

It was not long before the Princess was pouring out her tale of woe.

"Out every day with that Dandini. All he wants to do is to dress up in those stupid clothes and go to Balls. Do you know, I found him and that slug Dandini, in my bedroom wearing my best tights! They were dancing around the room slapping themselves on the thigh. He never helps me with the business. He's just off every day with that mincing, perfumed peacock Dandini. D'you know, his mother was a fairy." Cindy paused to dab her eyes.

Grunge hesitated. This was a difficult question. "Does he.... in bed? Does he er, how shall I put this? Does he perform his ah, princely duties?" Grunge felt his face flushing with embarrassment.

"Does He Perform His Princely Duties! No he does not! He slobbers all over my feet and that's it."

"That's it?" murmured Grunge. "Nothing else?"

"He's got a foot fetish. All he wants to do is kiss my feet. He doesn't think about My needs, My feelings, do you know he won't let me wear comfortable shoes! I have to wear too tight, too hard Bloody Glass Slippers!" Her voice diminished from a roar to a wail of despair. "I can't bloody walk. I'm getting bunions and I Have to wear bloody glass slippers."

When all the sobbing was spent and all the notes taken Grunge showed her to the door promising to give the matter urgent priority.

Over the next few weeks Grunge wrote several letters, assuring her that all processes were in hand. There were three more interviews at which Cindy sobbed and Grunge took copious notes. Wonderful!

thought Grunge. This is how the money rolls in!

To Cindy those few weeks seemed forever. On most days she visited her stepsisters, Hermione and Petal, at the health salon, not because she had any particular affection for them but because it gave her the excuse to wear tracksuits and divinely comfortable trainers. The resident chiropodist advised her that the glass slippers would cause untold problems in later life. She could not tell anyone that she was taking steps to eliminate the problem. At times, she felt envious of her ex ugly sisters. When Cinderella had become Princess Cindy and all were expected to live happily ever after, her Fairy Godmother, with a wave of her wand, had removed most of their disfiguring features. They were not beauties. Fairy Godmothers work magic, not miracles. They looked their best with the light behind them.

Grunge sent her another letter suggesting that she made an urgent appointment as matters had reached crisis point.

"It seems, ah, Cindy, that we have hit a major problem. I have drawn up pleas to the courts, listing grounds of unreasonable behaviour and demanding a huge cash settlement but," He paused, shuffling his papers. "But we do not have a court to whom we can apply. I have discovered that Happy Ever Aftia does not have one. There are neither criminal nor civil courts. I have searched every record," said Grunge, gesturing at the shelves of heavy books which lined the walls. "Nothing. I can do no more."

Grunge wondered if now was the time to raise the subject of his bill. Cindy's sobs seemed to indicate that it might be better to send the huge bill to her by post. At last he managed to persuade her to leave but only by promising to continue searching for a way out of her problem.

On Saturday Grunge decided to take the day off. He felt that he deserved the rest and was walking by a stream enjoying the peace. He realised how noisy the village was every day with the continual clatter of clogs on the cobbles and the incessant trivia of the villagers' happy chatter. The only other person in view was an old lady walking her aged dog.

"Good day, young man," she quavered. It was the Fairy Godmother (By Appt.)

Arthur made all the appropriate noises about what a lovely day it was and what a wonderfully intelligent little dog and turning to go, put his foot firmly into a deposit left by that dear intelligent dog! As he struggled to wipe his shoe clean he thought, it's all that stupid old woman's fault! And then he had a brilliant idea.

At home he sat at his desk. This would require careful thought. It would affect so many people. Yes. It would work. He would go for an Annulment on the grounds of non-consummation of marriage and he would appeal to the Fairy Godmother (By Appt.) She started it so she must finish it.

Arthur Grunge, Divorce Lawyer, sent a letter to the FGM (By Appt.) asking if she would call to see him at a mutually convenient time.

"So you see Godma'am, it is all your fault. Your magic has caused my client, The Princess Cinderella, grievous harm and she will look to you for restitution."

"But what can I do? I'm retired. I can't fly now you know. I get dizzy. It's the Vertigo." She paused and thought. If she could undo her "Good Deed" it would mean turning the clock back. In the process she too would turn back. She too would be younger. She would be rid of this nagging rheumatism.

"I'll do it," she said, rummaging through her bag. Shedding wool and knitting needles, she exhumed a battered wand and clearing her throat, she warbled,

> "Because of Cindy's tears,
> let us annul these past sad years."

The wand twinkled and Happy Ever Aftia swirled in a maelstrom of collapsing time...............

Cinderella sat beside the dying fire, toasting her pretty toes as she listened to the sounds of her Father, Stepmother, Hermione and Petal, leaving for the Ball. Buttons was making the cocoa and she was looking forward to a quiet evening when she and Buttons could dream their future.

The dark corner of the room lightened as the Fairy Godmother appeared. Cinderella sighed, what a time to have visitors! Just when she was having some peace and quiet.

"I am your Fairy Godmother. Tell me child, how can I help you to be happy?"

Cinderella took a deep breath. Chances like this come only once or maybe twice in a lifetime.

"Oh, Fairy Godmother, Buttons and I love each other. We want to get married."

"But how will you live, my child?"

Cinderella pulled from her apron pocket the cash flow and expenditure charts that she and Buttons had imagined.

"We have this dream of setting up a double glazing company, but we don't have the cash to start."

"Fetch me a pumpkin and six white rats," said the FGM. She did not know why but she vaguely remembered that that was the proper way to proceed. It was not easy but by using a doubtful rhyme she was able to compose a spelling charm in which Cinders was rhymed with winders.

The magic wand twinkled and the pumpkin became a factory on a brown field site and the six white rats became six of the finest double-glazing salesmen.

At the Ball Prince Charming was explaining to Dandini that people were beginning to talk.

"I really do not know was all the fuss is about, Dandy old chap but we need wives and as he spoke, Hermione and Petal made their entrance.

"I say Princy, look at those two old boots!"

It could not be said that it was love a first sight but the Prince knew that he could include an old boot in his foot fetish.

Arthur Grunge is back at University studying Sociology. He intends to become a social worker.

And they all lived happily ever after.

Psst

—◆—

"Psst." There it is again. Someone is trying to catch my attention. I look around. No one here, just all these smelly, mewing cats. I don't like cats but I've promised Gloria that I'd come to the PDSA to find a replacement for the dear departed Tibbles, beloved obsession of my Mother-in-Law also known as the Wicked Witch of West Ham. I look at a snarling, spitting, sharp tooth, hook claw, oversized kitten and think, perfect! They're made for one another.

"Psst," there it is again! I check around again. No; I'm all alone.

"For goodness sake come closer," hisses the large off-white ball of cotton wool in the next cage. I look a little more carefully. Dark pointed face, large round blue eyes and thick ivory coloured fur. "Listen" it snarls, I'm breaking all the rules by talking to you but I'm desperate."

"Yr, you're just a cat." I stammer.

"No I'm not JUST a cat, I'm Oscar. I'm a true bred, pedigree Burman and I'm in trouble, you've got to save me."

"B.. but cat's can't talk," I splutter. "If people see me talking to you they'll think I'm mad."

14

"Shut up and listen, there's not much time. I heard the Vet say that I'm due to be: Neutered!" he explodes. You've gotta get me outa here."

I'm too shocked to be rational. I slip a couple of pound coins in the collecting box, borrow a cardboard carrier and I'm back in my car.

"Well let me out of this bloody box will you! Treating me like a bloody animal!"

I drive to a quiet lay-by and open the box.

"That's better," says Oscar. "I suppose I owe you an explanation."

"First of all, yes, I can talk. All Burmans can talk. Many centuries ago we were called 'Temple Cats.' We were trained and taught to speak by Burmese monks but we were forbidden to speak to any other humans."

Oscar is now sitting on my lap in the driver's seat.

"Everyone thinks that our job in the temples was to look pretty and to kill the rats. That's rubbish. Well, of course we look exceedingly handsome but killing rats was a job for ill-bred moggies. Our job was far more important; As you know all cats have a natural Qi.."

"What's Qi?" I ask.

"Don't keep interrupting!" Says Oscar, digging his claws in to my thigh.

"As I was saying, all cats have natural Qi but we Burmans are the best." We're powerhouses of Qi. How can I explain." He sighs. "We just know where good energy exists in a home and that creates beneficial harmony."

He sees I've no idea what he's talking about but he sighs and carries on.

"Now, as I was saying; We Burmans were trained because of our natural ability and we advised on all matters of Feng Shui."

"I've heard of Feng Shui" I say. "That's where you make sure that furniture and things in the house are in the right place to make good vibes."

"SHUT UP," Shouts Oscar. "I've broken all the rules by talking to you and you will continue to interrupt.

"I lived with my Pet called Hetty who looked after my needs quite well but she tended to be rather irritable. As we lived alone I thought I could help by getting her mated. It was hard work at first. I had to get rid of the dustbin at the front door – it blocks Qi from getting in to the house. I persuaded Hetty that little crystals on strings hung at the windows were to stop me clawing the curtains. Absolute rubbish! Everyone with any sense knows that the crystals focus Qi within the room. Eventually I got the house perfect. As you say, 'good vibes' equals harmony equals fertility."

"It was easy to fix her up with a mate. I'd found him living alone just down the road. I would get "lost" time and time again and Hetty would always find me in Tom's garden."

"And then it all went wrong," Oscar gulps and seems to brush away a tear. "Tom moved in, Hetty got pregnant and Tom got asthma. I don't believe it really. I think he wanted to get rid of me because I usually sleep in Hetty's bed. I can't stand people who are so manipulative! Of course, if I had had the time I could have arranged for the block of flats on the other side of the road to be pulled down and the extra Qi would have really perked him up. But Tom blamed it all on my fur. I heard them talking, saying they would have to get rid of me. I can take a hint. I ran away, finished up in the PDSA where you found me."

"Excuse me for interrupting," I say. "But you're not out of the woods yet. "You'll be living with my Mother in Law and even the mention of her name gives me the shivers. You might enjoy the odd ride on her broomstick but she's vicious. She hates me, thinks I'm not good enough for her daughter. She hates all men and that includes you. Unless she gets you neutered." I say a little spitefully.

"Just leave her to me," says Oscar as he climbs back in to the box.

I get a bit of agro at home. Gloria says Mum wanted a black kitten and I've brought a white fur machine. I brush the front of my suit that has turned from blue to grey and bow my head beneath the onslaught.

Oscar behaves so well when I deliver him to the witch. He purrs and allows himself to be patted and stroked. I escape with just a few admonitions as to when I am going to get promoted, when am I going to buy her Glory a more suitable home and when if ever, can she expect to become a Grand Mother. I feel the knives in my back as I bravely turn to wave a fond farewell.

It must be about six weeks later when we finally get to visit Mother in Law again. Of course there have been several phone calls. It seems that Oscar is creating a disaster area. Her beautiful glass panelled plastic front door is ruined and has had to be replaced with a hard wood door. Curtains have been ruined, vases broken and all this chaos is heaped upon my head.

Gloria is parking the car so I approach the witch's lair alone. I listen, hoping she may not be in. I can hear a strange noise, unearthly, weird. I ring the bell on the handsome new door and there is a gentle chiming. She opens the door.

She is singing. So that's what the noise was! She's wearing a hint of make-up and she has had her hair done. More frightening still she is smiling. "Come in darling" she says. "Find yourself a nice seat. I'll put the kettle on."

Oscar is walking between my legs, leading me towards a soft chair in a room I hardly recognise. It's a transformation. So light, so airy. Gloria is in the kitchen with her Mother and Oscar is sitting on my lap.

"Oh, Oscar's letting you sit in his chair," trills my Mother in Law. "I've made your favourite cake, coffee and walnut. Here have a big piece. If you want another slice take it. You're looking a little pale, we'll have to fatten him up won't we Glory?"

Gloria explains that Mum says that we won't be able to stay long as Mum is expecting a friend for supper.

"It's such a surprise really," says Mum, "You see, one day last week

I couldn't find Oscar. I looked everywhere but I couldn't find him. Anyway, to cut a long story short, we found him stuck high up in a tree. I was beside myself but this gentleman that lives a bit down the road, got a ladder and climbed up and rescued Oscar. We got to talking and he is coming to supper this evening."

I swear Oscar winks at me.

As we leave and turn to wave I realise that Gloria and I are holding hands. Better yet, her hand feels so wonderful. We hurry home chattering just like old times. We have a little intimate supper for two and, in the morning, I enrol us both for a beginners' course of Feng Shui and in addition, I'm suggesting to Gloria that it would be really good if we had a cat of our own.

The Two Forty One at Kempton

— ◆ —

I watch the 2.30 race on the TV above the pub bar. Jimmy's horse trails in a tired fourth and I think that, now, Jimmy's really got problems. Outside the pub I duck under the wire and cross the racecourse car park. I look at my watch, twenty to three, just time for a quick leak behind the cars before I get back to work. Christ! I needed that! I zip up.

Clunk. I think that the car park is deserted but that was a car door shutting.

There it is. I see Jimmy about 50 yards away. That's a shotgun in his hands. He's going to top himself! I lurch into a run. I have to stop him. He's my best friend.

Jimmy Parkson and I both started as apprentices at the Grogan Stables some thirty years ago. We roomed together and covered for each other or, more usually, I covered for him when he stayed out late chasing, in turn, all three Grogan daughters.

We had both been reasonably successful on the flat but I had grown too heavy and after many jobs around the tracks, I now had the dubious distinction of being the entire reporting staff of "Racing Tips." Jimmy was more successful and rode three classic winners.

He's now struggling to make the grade as a trainer.

I try to shout to Jimmy to stop. I run as fast as my distended belly will allow me. I have to stop him. He is like the brother I never had.

I remember how, when we were both stable jockeys for Clare's he had spent all the hours when he was not working chasing and catching other people's girl friends, daughters, wives. He said that the activity kept his weight down and that he was such a good lover it was his duty to "Pleasure" as many fillies as possible. He did not always get away with it. I remember how one owner's wife wanted him, as he put it, "Exclusively" and the results had been, eventually a high profile divorce which made the headlines in all the racing papers.

I try to run faster. The liquid lunch of the day and too many days before, mean I'm carrying too much weight for the going. Kempton is a beautiful course but in the rain, all racecourses are the same; mud under foot and rain down the neck. I almost fall as my suede chukka boots slip in the greasy mud. Every moment stretches like a slow motion replay of the final straight. Every second slows to infinity.

Jimmy Parkson, ex-jockey, struggling trainer and my best friend is putting the muzzle of a shotgun into his mouth.

I remember how Jimmy always told me never to count the cost, take pleasures as they come and to hell with the consequences.

It has not always been fun for me. Jimmy would make his play for any girl friend that I may have had and there were very few of them! I thought of soft, gentle Joyce, who I had really loved. Jimmy had used all his charms, tricks and for her, unaccustomed drinks, to take her and then laugh at my pain.

I'm nearly there. The extra weight I'm carrying is taking its toll. I can feel the liquid in my stomach swilling around and rising in my throat. If I try to shout several pints of best bitter will re-appear.

I've got to stop him.

I have finally found a wonderful girl and I am now the proud father of a three-year-old son. I love John. He will be something good. Not a second rate jockey that I was nor the seedy reporter that I have become. He will be a son to be proud of.

I'm nearly there. He's got his thumb on the trigger. I see his clear green eyes staring blindly.

In that moment, almost within touching distance, I stop. My liquid load swishes slowly to a halt and I wait.

Jimmy pulls the trigger. I do not hear the sound of a shot but I think I hear a scream. I see Jimmy's face disappear in to mess of blood, bone and torn, shapeless flesh.

I'll never forget that bastards green staring eyes. I will see them every day when I look at my son John.

A Fish Called Boris

— ◆ —

Since the 'Days At sea' quotas have been severely depleted by the new fisheries agreement from the EU, our reporter has been visiting our fishing ports to see how the fishermen are coping with the reduced catches.

One such fisherman, a Mr. Sidney Flowerdew, in Grimsby has uniquely discovered a method of fishing requiring no 'days at sea' and the following interview describes our reporter's findings.

I found Mr. Flowerdew sitting in an old armchair on the Grimsby beach next to a large shed-like structure. I introduced myself and asked what he was doing.

"Waiting for t' tide to come in."

"So that you may launch your boat?"

"Na, the tide cum in, fills that gully and that fills me tank in t' shed then I close off t' tank."

"But, Mr. Flowerdew.."

"Call me Sid."

"Er, yes, Sid. But you can't get many fish that way."

"T' tanks 'eaving wif fish. I takes what I want and let the littleuns out darn the gully."

"That's amazing Sid, all those fish just swim up the gully?"

"Yers and then I feed Boris and then I'm off 'ome to watch Countdarn. 'Old on, tides nearly up to me chair. That's when I close off me tank. See what 'f caught."

We went in to the shed and found the tank full of writhing fish. Sid, pushed down a board which closed off the tank from the gully. I was surprised to hear Mr. Flowerdew, saying, "Well done Boris, that's a fine catch of bass."

"Mr. Flowerdew," I said, "Who's Boris and where is he?"

"'Ose Boris! Why, Boris is me secret weapon. 'Ere 'e is, in 'is own tank. Good boy Boris, 'ere's your favourite."

Mr. Flowerdew spread paste on small pieces of melba toast and dropped them in the tank. 'E loves Shippam's 'Am and Chicken paste and 'e don like it if the toast gets too soggy. There we are old chap. Good job done. Na' when you go out tomorrow I want good size Dover Soles they be fetching good prices."

I helped Sid load the fish in to fish boxes covered in ice and then loaded on to a small lorry.

Before leaving for the market Mr. Flowerdew explained the history of Boris.

"I was sitting 'ere playing me mouth organ when I sees this big dog fish lying in the shallows so I stops and fort I'd 'elp it back in to deeper water but as soon as I started playing 'e was back again. Anyrate, to cut a long story short I got to realize that 'e really liked, "I'm for ever blowing bubbles."

"Now, I interjected, you are going to tell me that Boris is West Ham supporter."

"Na." He continued, "I fink it's because 'e is."

"He is what?"

"'E is forever blowing bubbles. Well everyday I was on the beach blowing my Mouth Organ there 'e would be. One day 'e came and pushed on the beach a nice Dover Sole for me and I got to finking that maybe Boris could be like a sheep dog for me. So that's 'ow it all started. Boris is real smart and picks up quick everythink you say.

"And can Boris speak to you?" I ask.

"Na, cos not 'es only a bleedin fish!"

The Magic Carpet

——◆——

Alice Pryor felt old. She felt that life had passed her by and that now, on her sixtieth birthday, alone in this small dowdy house she was redundant. Looking back over her life she realised that, the cliché 'School days are the happiest days' was painfully true.

She had been a bright student with the expectation of good A level results and a place at university. She remembered how, each morning on her way to school she walked through the market square with her friends. Always the leader, carefree, and then she met John. He worked in the Butcher's shop and as the girls passed he raised his straw hat in mock gravity to say, 'Good morning ladies.' All the group would giggle, except Alice. She was quiet. Her friends teased her. 'Alice fancies him.' 'You just want some of his pork chops.' Alice did 'fancy him.' She began to stop at the shop on her way home from school and chat.

John had been working in the shop since he had left school but he told Alice that he had big plans. She loved him, believed him and willingly gave up all her own plans to marry him.

They rented a small, furnished flat. It was intended that Alice would find a job to help build a nest egg but, too soon, she found herself pregnant.

When Andrew was born Alice Pryor felt that life was just beginning and that the future was full of hope and love. The flat was her world and she spent her days making a home for her family.

John left the butcher's. There was, he said, no future in it. He had 'plans.' He had a telephone installed. He told her he had bought two hundred handbags from bankrupt stock and that they would need to sell them quickly before the bills fell due as all their money was in those bags. John spent his time on the telephone and Alice delivered bags in the pram with Andrew perched on top. In the evenings, between caring for John and Andrew, she used the telephone to generate more sales. It was, she thought, all worthwhile. She had complete faith in John and knew he would succeed.

They sold the bags and, with the profits, John bought a quantity of Chess Sets at a very low price. They proved more difficult to sell than the bags but Alice, with the telephone directory beside her, tirelessly worked, pleading, bargaining and selling. John bought cameras, golf balls, toys. John bought, Alice sold.

John began to describe himself as an 'entrepreneur.' He bought himself a smart suit, opened a small office with Alice to answer the phone and baby Andrew to keep her busy. When times were good John engaged a 'temp' and Alice spent time at the flat although John insisted that she stay close to the phone in case some deal should present itself.

Alice began to plan how she would have a lovely home when their 'ship came in.' She planned the curtains, carpets furniture, garden.

She planned a warm home for her family. There was a twinge of sadness that John had decreed that there would be no more children until the business was on a more secure footing.

When sales were slipping and stock and bills were a problem, Alice would take to the phone again and use every moment to make sales. She knew all the possible buyers by name and had built up an understanding with them so that she could get a sale where many would have failed. In any crisis, Alice would take a deep breath and meet it with fierce determination not to be beaten.

John bought a large modern apartment and Andrew went to an expensive school. 'No more children,' said John, 'Let's really do the best by Andrew.' Alice regretted not having a little sister or brother for Andrew and she would have preferred to live in a house. John said stated that a modern apartment was more suitable.

Even the furnishings were dictated by John. When Alice suggested a pretty chintz or a comfortable, homely chair John would appear to agree but Alice began to notice that her choices were not what was bought.

On occasions, when John was entertaining business friends, she observed, with a pin-prick of annoyance, that he would speak of himself as a 'self made man.' He would boast of the deals *He* had made and the fortune that *He* would make.

John insisted that Alice should remain close to home so that she would not miss the important deals that he preferred to negotiate away from the office. At times she wanted to be feel free, to go out for the day, anywhere, just to be Free.

Andrew was sent to boarding school. Alice wished for him to remain at home but John determined that Andrew was to have all the advantages that John had not had.

And then, at last, John announced that they were to buy a house, a large house in keeping with his position. Alice felt that this would make all those anxious years of working and sacrifice worthwhile. This was the dream fulfilled.

She did not like the house. John had chosen it and then taken Alice to see it. It was large, grand and draughty. Worse still, all the decisions that she so longed to make were made by an elegant young lady who John explained was an interior designer of great ability and prestige. Alice did not like her. She was gaudy, over painted and dropped her Ts. In her mind Alice summed her up as, 'A'll show and no knickers.' It was not a home. It was a Show House.

John bought Alice a mobile phone so that, he said, she would always be on hand but could go out more. Alice felt like a dog with the illusion of freedom when its master buys it a longer lead.

When Alice was fifty she felt empty. Andrew had grown up a stranger and had left England to settle with his new wife in America and John seemed to spend more time away on business. She wondered if he was being unfaithful but she felt powerless, helpless, alone.

It was, she thought, time to make a life for herself. Perhaps she could enroll for some evening classes and at least get out of the house for a time. She studied the list from the local Adult Education

Centre and was torn between so many choices. Eventually it was Hobson's as the only course with places still available was Philosophy. She had only a distant memory of what Philosophy meant but she paid her fee and enrolled. John thought the idea was hilarious but agreed that, if she would go by bus, he would collect her and bring her home.

The class consisted of a mixed group of students with an elderly tutor. Jane felt young and to her surprise, found herself hotly discussing and disputing. Happy, in a way that she had not been since she left school she would leave the class flushed with pleasure. But she did not enjoy being collected by John. She had tried to tell him of her small triumphs but John would pinprick her pleasure with condescending laughter. Alice told John that he was much too busy to be tied to collecting her. She would arrange for a taxi.

It was always the same man, Arthur. He was about sixty and as the weeks passed, she learnt how he has been made redundant, how along with the loss of his job, his wife had left him and how he now lived in two rooms. 'It don't matter,' he said because he was out most evenings in the car and he just needed somewhere to sleep, have the odd meal and do a bit of washing. 'So,' he said, 'I don't get lonely, there's often nice people to talk to in the cab.' Alice felt sure that this was a gentle complement.

John told her that he wanted a divorce. He had been seeing another woman for some time and he wanted to marry her. Alice found out later that the lady in question was the same, still elegant woman, who had 'created' her house all those years ago. John said *He* would give her enough money to get her settled and that he intended to move 'Gloria' in to *His* house.

Alice felt stunned but inside herself she could feel a voice of protest. *He* would *give* her! Surely he was only giving her what she had earned during all those years. She had helped with his career and surely the house that John stated as *His* was also *Hers*.

Her solicitor was young, nervous and useless. Somehow, all the money that John had boasted of now vanished. The house was, it seemed, in the Company's name and he declared few assets of his own. Alice's solicitor seemed to think that she should be grateful for the money that her husband was prepared to *Give* her.

The final settlement was that she would have enough money to buy a small house and a little income to supplement her forthcoming old age pension. Andrew, her son, now in Australia, wrote her letters begging her to be careful with her money. Alice could also read the lines that he did not write, 'You are really not competent to look after yourself and I don't want the responsibility. Dad was probably right to leave such a little mouse as you and find himself someone more stimulating and more suitable to his position.'

She did not feel at home in the small house she had bought. The furniture had been grudgingly given to her by John and were probably the pieces that were not to Gloria's taste. The curtains and carpets were left by the previous owner and Alice felt a lodger in what should have been her home. She did very little. She shopped, she cleaned, she read the papers. She did not go to philosophy classes.

The bold print in the local paper caught her attention:

Grand Carpet Sale
Bankrupt Stock
Sale By Auction
Un-Repeatable
BARGAINS.

It stirred her imagination. She would go and buy, for herself, a carpet that she liked.

'Lot 48,' shouted the auctioneer. 'Fine colourful twist-weave all wool carpet. Twelve yards, three yards wide. Beautiful colours.' Silence:

'Look at those colours! You could drop a three course meal on that and not notice it.' There was a dutiful splatter of laughter and finally it was sold. Alice did not care. She had been given a large numbered card, when she came in and, as soon as she had seen it, she knew which carpet she wanted. Not lot 48 with its wonderful colours nor lot 63 which the auctioneer said, to another ripple of laughter, that it was so cheap he thought to buy it himself for the garage.

Alice knew what she wanted. Lot 103 described as 'Crimson and Black Patterned, Wilton Type, Wool Carpet.'

'Lot 103,' shouted the auctioneer. 'Fine carpet, you could bleed to death on that and no-one would notice.' He waited for the dutiful titter. The jokes were wearing thin and Alice felt angry that he should be making fun of *her* carpet.

'Who will start the bidding at 200?' There was a silence. Alice lifted her card.

'Thank you Madam. Anyone make it 250? Thank you Sir. 300? Thank you Madam. 350, 400, 450... It's with you Madam. 500, Thank you, 600...' Alice bought it for £800 plus 10% buyer's fee and VAT. It was far more that she had intended to pay but it was hers.

At the back of the hall, as she prepared to leave was a tall mournful looking man who gave her a card. He was, it informed, a reliable, inexpensive carpet layer of many years experience.

'Can you lay my carpet for me? Can you collect it and lay it for me?'

'Course I can, it's me job in'it? Give you a special price... I'll do a good job Missus.'

Alice felt sorry for him. He seemed so thin and his eyes seemed crossed so that it was never certain where he was looking. The knees of his trousers and his jacket cuffs were frayed.

When the details and payments had been concluded Alice went back to her house. She could not sleep. She was too excited.

She had arranged for the carpet to be delivered and fitted the following Wednesday morning and only then did she realise that she also had an appointment to see her GP.

She let him in. 'Look,' she said, I've got to go out for a while. Will you be all right to leave you to it? Shouldn't be long.'

'Course s'orlrigh'. Let the dog see the rabbi'.

The Doctor was running late and then had insisted on giving a lengthy lecture on how he was reluctant to continue to prescribe the anti-depressants she had come to rely on since her divorce and that she ought to pull herself together. Alice took her prescription. The buses were delayed and it was well over two hours since she had left home.

He was just finishing. 'There y're Mum. I've made a goo job though as I sez it m'self. You 'ad a bi' left over so I fort I'd lay it in the 'all. 'ope that's all right.' Finally he left, heartily thanked and paid.

Alice Pryor sat in her Home looking at her carpet. It sang. It warmed her. She cried not with pain but with joy. She was home. She thought she would start evening classes again. She would need to book a taxi to bring her home. Perhaps she would invite Arthur in for a cup of tea.

Alice Pryor

— ◆ —

I wanted to be at the crematorium before the hearse so I hurried ahead. I was curious to see who would come, if any. God! I don't like these places. I can see that this one has facilities for four simultaneous services. I check the typewritten list. Alice Sheila Pryor, room C, 10.15. There is a large clock above the list showing that there is more than half an hour to wait. I move to reception area C. There's just one chap sitting there all by himself. Dejected, with elbows on knees and head bowed. Good Lord! It's Arthur. I didn't recognize him. He looks so different in a suit and neatly combed hair. I sit next to him and want to put my arm around him but that is not possible.

Hullo! Here comes someone else. I do not see very clearly. I seem to see through a watery film. Maybe I'm crying. Perhaps it's Andrew. I do hope so, all the way from America. No it's Mr. Starbuck. I thought for a moment he was going to sit on me but he's moved to the other side. He's going to talk to Arthur.

"Excuse me, is this the right place for the Alice Pryor funeral? Or am I too late. I was not sure of the time."

"No mate, I mean yes. This is the place but there is still half an hour to go. Er, are you a relative of Alice, I mean Mrs. Pryor?

"No, not a relative, just, I hope, a friend. You?"

Nah, I'm not even a friend but well, I had to come. I drive a mini-cab you see and on an off, for about 2 years now, I've collected her from her evening classes. We used to talk and I dunno, she was such a nice lady that I had to come. She was so full of life and I dunno, I can't put it in to words. I just so enjoyed our little chats." Oh Arthur, I thought, so did I.

"Well, we seem to have so much in common. My name's Starbuck, Phil Starbuck. I am, I mean, was, the lecturer at those evening classes and yes, she was a remarkable woman. She had such vivacity, such a young enquiring mind. She was, I think, so er, lovable."

I could see Arthur nodding. I wanted to tell them to cheer up but I think we all sat there with tears blurring our vision.

There's another couple coming. Perhaps it's Andrew and he's brought his girl friend. No, it's just James and that slut Gloria. He looks smart enough, though he's put on weight but Angela! What does she look like, mutton dressed up as lamb. Not suitable for any funeral, let alone mine. What a bloody cheek, he's on his mobile:

"No, Andrew, it's perfectly sensible of you not to come, I mean all the way from America. It's a waste of time and money. Right, right! I'm just putting in an appearance. I'll ring you later."

He told Andrew not to come! You pompous load of shit!

"Ange, go back and sit in the car and wait for me. Take the phone

36

idiot! You know you've got to be on hand in case I get a message about the Filton contract."

God, that takes me back, I think. Just like me she's got to be there to do what he wants and get no thanks for it.
James sits down next to Mr. Starbuck.

"This is right for the Pryor funeral is it?"

"Yes, mate, we've got about another 15 minutes to wait. You a relative?"

"Well er, yes. I am, I mean, was her husband. We've been divorced now for over two years but I thought I should put in an appearance. Though it's hard to spare the time. I'm negotiating a very valuable government contract and well, I have to admit, it's on a knife edge."

And, I thought, I bet you paid out more money than you have, to grease a few palms as you claw your way over the opposition. One day Mr. Self-made bloody James Pryor you'll get your comeuppance.

There are just a few more people showing up. Not many. Look there are Joan and Sylvia from the class. Oh! that's kind of them to come and Mr. Willis from next door.

And now, that's Gloria running back waving the phone.

"James, James, they've made the announcement."

James grabs the phone;

"Hullo, yes yes, who got it? Waltons!" he exploded. "The mean conniving bastards! All that money and sod all to show for it!"

He looks quite ashen, distraught, just like a husband should look at his wife's cremation. I think I'm going to enjoy my funeral.

The Donkey

—— ◆ ——

Sometimes, now I'm rescued, I just stand here looking over the fence at the traffic roaring by and ponder on the meaning of life. I mean, what's it all about? What is my purpose in life? Why am I here?

I never knew my Mum. She was taken away almost as soon as I was born and the nearest I ever had to a Mum was Mr. Grisewold feeding me with my bottle. There were just 10 of us then. I was the smallest of course and at first, too weak to carry the children so I would just stand on the beach, wearing a stupid hat with holes cut for my ears, and have my photograph taken with the children. When I got bigger, I got a saddle and I could carry the smallest children a short walk up and down the beach.

Now, that was not a bad life in the summer but when winter came, we spent all the time crowded in the sheds. We all had our birthday at the same time. It was the spring day when Mr. Grisewold would lead us from the shed in to the little green, oh so green field where we ran, jumped and chewed fresh green green grass.

When we all had our strength back and the holidays were started, we each morning, were led to the beach to start work. I lost count of the years. I became the biggest and strongest and took the heaviest loads.

I can still see him. Mr. Grisewold was doubtful but agreed to let me take him. How shall I describe him? In a word, Fat! Skimpy bathing trunks almost concealed by folds of fat. It was hot and I fancied a lick of the ice cream he held in his hand. When he got on I felt a sort of click in my hindquarter but I adjusted to the weight and set off. We had gone but a short distance when my hip seemed to give way and I fell sideways spilling that great fat lump.

That was the end of my career. At first Mr. Grisewold said that I would have to be put down as the vet said I had a displaced hip and could not carry loads anymore. The RSPCA rescued me and I was re-homed here with Hilda.

Hilda lives in that house down there. She means well. She comes to talk to me most days and always makes sure I'm fed and watered but it's a lonely life.

Some mornings, to cheer myself up, I would sing but the people in that house, over there, said it was a terrible row and I was moved further from their house. I sometimes wish Mr. Grisewold had had me put down. I mean, what is the purpose to my life?

Ah! Here's Hilda now and she's not alone! She's brought a giant with her! Whatever it is, it is a big as 10 donkeys.

It's all right. Hilda has explained that Gordon is a Clydsdale who used to pull a beer carts and now he's redundant and lonely and I'm going to look after him. Now I can be useful. I can be a good companion to Gordon and he will be good for me. I mean, when it rains I can shelter from the rain by standing underneath him.

Chimp in a Spin

————◆————

"Dear Prime Minister
My name is Fryday. I'm a chimp."
No, that won't work. I'd better start again.

"Dear Prime Minister
I wish to resign my position as your Special Advisor to enable me
to spend more time with my family."

No, that won't work either. He thinks Marion is his chief spin
doctor. This is getting much too complicated. I think I will just tell
it as it is.

I was born in Regents Park Zoo. Everybody says I was a lovely
baby, a bit unusual perhaps, my fur had a tinge of green. My Mum
and I used to spend many hours laughing at the antics of the
humans that came to visit us. I sometimes wish that life had stayed
that way and that I had never met Marion. She was an Animal
Behaviourist and I started showing off because she had nice legs
and a pretty face. She had got permission to visit the Zoo after
hours to carry out tests on me. It got to the point where she was able
to take me away for special study.

I did not like to leave my Mum. I remember asking her why I was called "Fryday" and she dabbed away a tear and said that it was out of respect for my Uncle Louie.

Marion and I lived together to a pent house apartment overlooking Green Park. At first she taught me to recognise pictures and rewarded me with bits of bananas but I soon got fed up with that. I began to read and write but, sadly, I never was able to speak. I developed a taste for jellied eels, mussels, cockles and cuttle fish bone, that sort of thing.

I was Marion's big secret. I was to be a secret until her thesis was written and published and then we would be famous.

As I said, Marion was a pretty little thing so it was no surprise that she hooked up with Adrian, a young politician.

I was, of course, reading all the newspapers, watching the television and able to write memos that Marion passed on to Adrian as useful pointers.

Things like, colour of shirt, how to comb his hair and phrases such as: "This government is riddled with sleaze and I will not rest until it is swept away."

Adrian and Marion's affair cooled but Adrian prospered and when his party was swept to power he became a junior minister and Marion was appointed his special advisor.

I arranged, through Marion, to get my Mum retired to Whipsnade and I often used to visit her in the ministerial car with tinted windows. It was there I met and married Alice who has sustained me through this difficult period.

Adrian made meteoric progress with Marion's/my help. I created such phrases as; "The mess we inherited from the previous government." And; "Prudence, prudence and yet more prudence."

When the next election gave them an increased majority Adrian became Foreign Secretary and Marion was appointed special advisor to the Prime Minister. They were such wonderful exciting times. Marion and I advised the P.M. on how to brush his hair, when to take off his jacket, when to take off his tie, when to drink tea from a mug, when to smile. These were dizzy times, exhilarating.

I am very proud to have created such mantras as; "Which we inherited from the previous administration," and:

"The government has got a very exciting plan." And;

"For this reason the government has given X billions of pounds of new money." And best of all;

"The government has saved, by these cut-backs, X billions of pounds of tax-payers money."

But it has all now got to come to an end. I feel too insulted to carry on.

I talked this over with my Mum and Alice when I spent last weekend with them. They support me and agree that the insult to we chimps cannot be overlooked. I now wish to remain in retirement at Whipsnade, enjoy my family and maybe, write a few plays. My Mum finally told me about Uncle Louie. It seems, when she lived at Regents Park, Uncle Louie and she were good friends and she said, "I was lonely, Uncle Louie was older and wiser." She couldn't say any more but I thought she was blushing a little.

She did say something like, "I was just a chimp and he was a bright green parrot." On the day that I was born Mum says, Uncle Louie flew through the restaurant kitchen window, knocked over the hot chip pan and died a horrible death.

My Mum still cries when she talks of it and says, "You were called Fryday as a mark of respect for your dear Uncle Louie."

But that is bye the bye. I have to resign to uphold the honour of we chimps. I came across the following leaked memo that is short and to the point.

"The Prime Minister's Special Adviser is an Ass."

Yours respectfully…

"Hope Springs"

— ◆ —

Nearly everyone told Hope what a lucky girl she was. There would be no hard times at the start of her married life. Richard was the only son of George Springs who had years before, built up his little shop to become the large departmental store. "Springs" catering to the best families in town. Food department, Fashion, Furniture, Linen. There was even a small department supplying screws, nails, bits of wire, hardware, a token to the imposing store's humble beginnings. Dick Springs aged only twenty-eight, was in full charge, George having decided that he and his wife should enjoy the fruits of their good fortune while there was still life to enjoy.

Nearly everyone said Hope was a lucky girl except perhaps her Art teacher, Mrs Holmes who murmured that Hope should achieve the good A level she deserved rather than this rush to get married when she was only eighteen.

Hope had not listened. Dick, ten years her senior, had swept her off her feet and would not allow any delay. Dick was used to having his own way.

Life had been good. Richard Springs had bought for his young bride, a large house furnished to the highest standards by "Springs" The gardens were maintained by "Springs" garden centre and Hope had only to lift the phone for the food hall to deliver whatever she wished.

Just when perhaps the undemanding life was beginning to drag, Hope became pregnant and Fleur was delivered to the nursery, designed by the "Baby Care Consultant" in "Springs" Young Mother's Department.

For some time after the birth of Fleur, Hope was depressed. The Doctors made encouraging noises about postnatal depression,

"Quite common, it will pass. Just take it easy."

Dick showered Hope and Fleur with everything that "Springs" and money could buy. Hope loved her baby with a fierce love and threw off her depression by devoting all her energies to the needs of Fleur.

Richard Springs was used to the best. He had wanted Hope to employ a Nanny for Fleur but Hope would not agree. It was the only time that Richard allowed Hope to act for herself. In all other matters Richard would call on the relevant expert to make informed decisions on behalf of his child bride and sometimes, at night, as she lay awake, Hope would wonder if she were capable of anything other than to love and care for her baby.

But it is a fact of life that babies tend to grow and Fleur did. An enchanting toddler gave way to an assertive two and three year old and then, to Hope's secret dread, there came the day when Fleur was old enough to go to school.

Fleur loved school and Hope hated it. How could she fill her days without Fleur to care for? She tried to talk to Richard, could she get a job? Was there something she could do at the store? Richard laughed and patted her head.

"What could you do Baby? You don't need to work. You just stay here and be my beautiful wife."

Hope felt lost. It is one thing to live a life of ease but that is not the same living a life of Nothing to Do.

At the bottom of the garden was the Garage. In the time of the previous owners it had been the Chauffeurs cottage with housing for the car on the ground floor and living quarters above. The garage had been empty for many years and had fallen in to disrepair but Hope began to make her plans.

"You know the old Garage, Dick? Could I have it? I want to do it up and perhaps do a little painting down there. Turn it in to a sort of studio."

"Of course you can Baby" said Richard. "Just say what you want and I'll get some men to fix it for you."

"No" exclaimed Hope. "I just want to potter about a bit by myself. I don't want any help. I shall enjoy messing about with it.."

Richard could not understand why she would not want any help but if it would keep her happy then there was no harm in it and he could always get some men to fix it at a later date. Hope went to the Bank and opened an account. The Bank Manager seemed amused that she would want an overdraft but did not hesitate to grant it. In the town "Springs" was all the security he needed.

Hope checked over her new property. It seemed surprisingly sound. There was a damp patch in the upstairs living rooms but from the outside Hope could see two slipped tiles. She got a ladder, the roof was not too high, clambered across the roof and slipped the tiles back in to place. She was pleased to get back down to the ground but she felt exhilarated, as though she had conquered some high mountain peak.

The walls were rough plaster and after repairing the various cracks with filler she thought the walls ready for painting. She did not go to "Springs" for the emulsion. She went out of town. It took two visits. The first was to return with colour charts, which she pinned on the walls and considered in the changing light and then, decisions, made, she bought her paints, rollers and brushes.

 Richard wanted to come and see how she was getting on. He wanted to help. He wanted to get help but she would not let him come.

"Let me finish it first," she begged. "I want to see if I can do it for myself."

It was not easy. One of the walls needed plaster patching but she went back to her, out of town store and got advice from the salesman.

"Just read the instructions on the bag" he said vaguely.

Hope bought a bag, trowel and more brushes.

She did it. It was harder work than she had imagined. At first the plaster would not stay where she put it. She re-read the instructions and found that it may be easier if the walls were dampened.

She found then, that if she worked hard and fast, it would stay in place and as it dried she felt happy with the result.

The painting was fun and very satisfying. The old rooms seemed to come alive with the fresh colour.

In the local paper she saw an advertisement for an auction of carpets. She did not tell Richard. He would have merely arranged for his carpet department to advise and supply. Hope did not want that.

The auction was exciting and Hope felt she had got a bargain. Enough carpet for the entire property and the promise that a man would be in touch to come and lay it for her.

It was not until the carpets had been laid that Hope realised how effective all her efforts had been. It filled her with greater confidence to move on. She bought second hand curtains. Perfect! She went to another auction and bought for just a few pounds two painted bookcases which when stripped proved to be old oak, which just needed a little waxing.

She found a dilapidated Victorian Chaise- Longue and re-upholstered it. Hope went to many auctions and seemed able to buy for just a few pounds other peoples rubbish that with a little attention, became beautiful.

The intended studio was not a studio. It became almost a show

49

room of recovered treasures. Hope allowed Richard to come and
see her finished effort.

"Well done Baby" he exclaimed. "You've really done very well"
How much did it all cost.?"

"Well nothing" said Hope. "Some of the pieces I bought I did not
really need so I did them up and put them back in to auction and I
made a small profit enough to clear my overdraft"

Hope continued to go to auctions buying and sometimes selling.

It was a painting that finally set her on her way. She bought it for
ten pounds when no one else seemed to be interested. She sold it
for four hundred pounds just a few weeks later.

Hope showed Richard the little leaflet. It read;

"HOPE SPRINGS"
*"If you know what you want but cannot find it do not give up.
We undertake to search on your behalf and find just what
you need"*
*There was then a list of example items; a carver chair;
plates to match those from a broken dinner set; furniture;
old silver; porcelain figurines.......*
*"Hope Springs" did not make a fortune but it kept Hope
busy and content.*

One day Richard came home early.

"Baby, I wonder if you could spare a little time to come back to

'Springs' with me. I want you to look at the new layout of the soft furnishing department. I know it is just not right but I can't quite put my finger on it. Will you come and give me your opinion?" Hope smiled. Maybe Richard would stop calling her "Baby" .

Spread a Little Sunshine

— ◆ —

I used to watch BBC 1 all the evening because my remote control was on the blink and it was too much of an effort to get out of the chair to change channels. I'm a different man now I've got it fixed. I can change channels with a flick of the finger. I'm sure it's been good for me. My finger is now fitter than ever.

My idea of exercise is re-stocking the fridge with several 6-packs of lager. After such exertions I usually lie on the couch for an hour or so, checking the quality of my purchases. I live alone and work from home. Each weekday, I roll out of bed, shower always, breakfast and take my morning exercise. It must be a brisk walk of three or four yards to my computer room. The morning's work is hectic. Some days I can be buying and selling shares until at least midday with only the briefest stops for, tea and biscuits and calls of nature. I rest a little over lunch and then trudge back to my computer room to check the progress of my morning decisions. It might be a little lonely but it suits me.

My polite friends have suggested that I should take more exercise and less food and drink. My mother, who did not know the meaning of the word "Polite" said, "You're like a beached whale and if you don't shape up and move your arse you'll need extra scaffolding on your computer chair."

My mother was a very devious woman. She got herself a year old Alsatian dog and then, not six months later, she died. I miss her very much; She was, I think, my best friend.

But life must go on. I inherited several handsome debts and an unruly, exercise needy, dog called Sunshine. We were not a perfect match. I had brought Sunshine home on the back seat of my car. I think the arm- rest that he ate, did not agree with him. I have a large plot of land behind my house that I have nurtured to become a wild garden – well that's my story! I thought that Sunshine may feel the need to water and fertilise and so I introduced him to the jungle while I unloaded the car with such essential doggy items as, basket, biscuits, blankets, bones and the rest of the alphabet.

I decided that, after such exertions, I needed recovery time and I had just settled on the couch with a mist covered, cool can of lager when I heard a hammering. By the time I had located the sound and opened the back door Sunshine had already reduced his side of the door to long slivers of wood littering the floor. Sunshine pushed by me. Young Alsatians seem to have enormous feet, an un-controlled tail and a large turning circle. These three, uncoordinated factors, destroyed the casual chaos of my kitchen. I put down a bowl of water. With load, slurping noises, Sunshine sprayed the floor. Finally Sunshine fell asleep, strategically stretched out in front of the computer room door. A man of my girth does not easily leap over a recumbent Alsatian but I did.

Later, when Sunshine awoke, refreshed, I tried re-introducing him to the garden but he would not budge. I thought I might be able to drag him out if I put him on his lead but the sight the lead turned him from a stubborn donkey to a whirling dervish and so began my drudgery. I had to take Sunshine for a W. A. L. K.

On the lead Sunshine is an irresistible force and I, at the other end, am a slow moving mountain. Something had to give and I think it was my shoulder. This was the start of a life of hell. W.A.L.Ks morning and evening. All doors in the house to remain open or face destruction and worst of all, Sunshine would only settle at night at the bottom of my bed.

We did settle to a sort of routine. The start of the day was a brisk tow around the park. Somebody said, I think, that if you want to make friends, get a dog. It is true. I found other strange companions willing to pass the time of day and exchange compliments about their respective dogs.

Sylvia was not a dog walker she was a jogger. It was Sunshine who effected the introductions. As Sylvia ran by, Sunshine contrived to entrap her with the lead. One apology led to a laugh and one laugh led to another, the results of which was that I was comfortably seated on a park bench while Sylvia bounded off with Sunshine scampering behind her. It was a most pleasant half an hour watching Sylvia and Sunshine lapping by.

Sylvia is a joy to describe. Not too tall; a neat figure – a credit to her jogging; long blonde hair worn in a pony-tail which bounced provocatively as she ran; and wide blue eyes. We got to be friends, morning and evening we would meet in the park and when Sylvia and Sunshine were exercised, I would produce a thermos flask of coffee – "No sugar thank you," and we would sit, talk and put the world to rights. Like me, Sylvia was lonely. She had first come to London a year ago to live with her student boy friend but it hadn't worked out. Like me, she was now an orphan but her parents had left her a comfortable inheritance, which enabled her to buy her own house and follow her dream to be a writer.

One morning Sylvia did not appear. I worried. Sunshine and I missed her very much. I had come to rely on seeing her trim little figure jogging to meet us and it made me realise how much I needed her. I was happy and relieved to see her bouncing towards us that evening. She said how sorry she had been to miss us but she had been out with a friend the previous evening and had not returned until the early hours of the morning and so she had slept in.

I felt a twinge of anxiety. Who was this friend? Was he a He? Would our little routine be brought to an end? I felt I must act quickly.

I was up early the next morning; showered and shaved, clean shirt, shiny shoes and new jacket. Sunshine was brushed until his coat shone and I managed to clean his teeth. We looked, I thought, good.

My hand was shaking as I poured out the coffee for Sylvia. She was prettily flushed from her exercise and the morning sunlight glinted on her hair. She listened to my proposal with what seemed a little surprise and perhaps she seemed a little sad. I hastened to tell her not to give me an answer but to think about it and give me her answer when we met in the evening.

That evening Sylvia said, "Yes"

Sometimes I still get up early in the morning. I sit at the window and watch Sylvia and Sunshine jog by. They seem made for each other.

I am trying a recipe for cornflakes with lager for breakfast. It saves the need for milk.

The Ten Pound Note
— ◆ —

Money was always a very important consideration for the Frost family or rather, the lack of it. Angela's husband, John was a bank clerk and his earnings were barely enough to pay the mortgage of the little bungalow in which they lived. What was left had to cover housekeeping, clothes, bills and more bills.

John's work in the bank presented an extra source of pressure. A bank clerk is expected to manage his own finances and whereas the manager might look kindly on an unauthorised temporary indiscretion by a bank customer, Angela and John were both painfully aware that alarm bells would ring if their account should fall from grace.

Each month presented new demands and challenges. Each month created new stresses within the family. Neither Angela nor John had any surviving close relatives who might provide an injection of cash or the hope of a small inheritance.

Jane, their eldest, was eleven, John Junior was nine and Joyce, the baby, was just five. All three children were well aware that demands for sweets or ice cream were often the start of discord between their parents. The lack of spare money was a big black cloud every day.

Angela knew that John loved her and the children but she also knew that the constant money worries created outbursts of anger and frustration as they battled to make ends meet. The lack of spare money was a big black cloud every day and for them, there was no hope of a silver lining.

Now that the children were all at school Angela knew that soon she would have to find some part time work to lighten the load but she had delayed this step until Joyce became more settled with her school life.

But there was joy in their children. Parents' evenings were their "Pay Back." Teachers praised the skills of Jane and John Junior and Baby Jo's teacher told them, in strictest confidence, that she did not have favourites but that, if she did then Jo would be the one. After such meetings the clouds rolled back a little with just the hope of happiness to come.

It was the start of the Autumn term when John Junior excitedly announced that he had been picked to play the lead role in a musical play to be put on by the school. As the term passed by Angela and John found themselves involved in making the stage costumes that were required for the production. Neither had any dress making skills but night after night, they stitched, unpicked and finished in time. Both Angela and John helped Junior learn his part and when the big day came, all the Frost family were word perfect for Junior's role. There were two performances and the Frost family proudly attended both.

As Angela watched John Junior she felt such pride and joy. She could feel tears pricking the corners of her eyes and her heart thumped within a strangely tight chest. Her lips moved to mirror every word that Junior sang. She looked at John and saw his face glowing with joy. All the players were good but Angela thought that Junior was by far the best. Junior looked so handsome and the hours of sewing were rewarded. At that moment there were no clouds just a perfect joy.

When Angela and John had first married John had been a medical student and Angela a staff nurse. They had great plans for the future secure in the knowledge that two could live as cheaply as one. Life decreed otherwise. Within a year of their marriage, Jane was born.

John would always remember the telephone call to the college. "Your wife has had a little baby girl. They are both fine. Oh, and by the way, when you come, your wife says for you to bring a tin of talcum powder." He borrowed the money from a fellow student for the bus fare and the tin of powder.

It was as he held the baby for the first time that he made up his mind that he would no longer be a student. He would get a job. His wife and baby needed so many things and he would get them for her. He made up his mind in that moment, that he would never allow himself to feel of express regret for the loss of his ambitions. He would be a loving father and that was the greatest prize.

Total security was a job in a bank.

As they walked home from the school with John Junior still proudly wearing traces of grease paint, both Angela and John found it difficult to express to their son how proud they felt. Words seemed inadequate.

Angela lay awake thinking how best she could show Junior how much she loved him and in the morning, she told John what she had decided. John's reaction at first, was to doubt if they could afford it. Angela said that it was not a matter of "Afford" but a recognition that must be made. She produced, from the inside pocket of her only coat, a little purse in which she kept her "Rainy Day Savings" From the thirty pounds she selected a ten pound note.

After breakfast Angela and John kept their son in the kitchen while the girls played in the sitting room. "We thought" said Angela, "That the play was lovely and that you, Junior, were really good. Daddy and I are so proud of you that we want you to have this for yourself to do what you want with it." She took out the ten pound note and gave it to him. "You worked really hard and we know that you deserve this."

"I think you had better open a savings account with it," said John but Angela was insistent. No, it's for Junior to do with as he wants. It is his and we can trust him."

Junior was stunned. He had never held so much money and with all the tensions that money caused in his family he knew that this was a significant moment. He began to put the note in his pocket when his Father said that perhaps they should look after it for him in case he should lose it. "No," his Mother said, "It is his and I know he will be sensible."

It was a wet Sunday morning with a strong wind blowing . John Junior wanted to walk round to the next road to see if his friend was in. Probably he just wanted to show him the ten pound note. He returned within an hour, crying and in an agony of convulsive sobs, gulped out that he had lost the money. It had been in his pocket when he left and "It was gone." John's first reaction was to tell Angela, "I told you so. You should not have let him keep the money."

Angela was not sure what was the real reason for going out. Maybe it was because she could not bear to see her son so upset. More likely it was because she hated to think that John had been right and that she should not have trusted Junior with the money but the reason she gave was she would go out and see if she could find the ten pound note. After all, she did know where Junior had walked.

The streets were deserted. A cold wet wind blew in to her face and she felt the damp soaking through her coat. The rows of bungalows seemed cheerless and Angela felt that the black cloud which always seemed over her head had finally burst. She could not go back to face the "I told you so," which would greet her. Water, tears or rain, streamed down her face. So blurred was her sight that she nearly bumped in to a car parked on the grass verge. "If only," she thought, "Someone could just give me the price of that car! I would lose all my worries and life would be sweet."

It was about ten minutes later when Angela returned triumphant, clutching a sodden ten pound note. "That was really lucky," she explained. "I found it stuck almost under the wheel of a car parked on the verge in a muddy puddle, so it had not blown away."

It was about two weeks later when the weather turned cold again and Angela instructed her brood to wrap up well on their way to school. As he set off, Junior decided to put on his gloves. He had books to carry and the icy wind nipped his fingers. He pushed his hand into the scrunched up woollen glove and found, carefully folded in to a small square, the lost ten pound note which he now remembered he had put there for safety.

Woof

— ◆ —

At some time in the past my bedroom ceiling had been papered with a heavily embossed, random squiggled paper. I suspect that this had been done to cover up the fact that the original plaster was badly cracked. I liked my ceiling. When I lie in bed I could look up and imagine pictures made by the whorls and dents. My bedside light cast shadows making my own picture gallery. There was a lady in perhaps a crinoline dress, there a horse jumping over a hedge, there a large dog with big ears and an elephant standing in a bowl of water. It got so that, every night, before I switched off the light I would re-imagine my pictures.

I fell asleep one night, failing to switch off the light and I awoke at the sound of a strange noise. The dog on my ceiling was turning its head towards me and instead of the black and white line drawing, the dog was becoming grey- brown. It seemed to grow out of the ceiling and land lightly at the foot of my bed.

"Good," it said, "I'm glad you've finally decided to wake up. I've been trying to get your attention ever since you moved in."

I could not move. I was too petrified to speak. I dare not breathe.

"Come on man!" it said, "pull yourself together. You're not in any danger. You are just experiencing your first trance. Relax, take a few deep breaths and listen. My name is Chimbu and I am your spirit guide. I knew as soon as you moved in that you were a psychic and even more special, you were a psychic path to the dog after-life. We will do great things together. Look! switch the light out, go back to sleep. I'll come a see you soon when you have got your mind round the fact that you are a medium.

It's all a dream, I thought and switched off the light.

By the morning I had almost forgotten my dream but as I fluffed up my duvet, to make my bed I did notice a patch grey-brown spiky hairs near the bottom. Come on, Charlie, I thought, don't let your imagination run away with you.

Yes, that's me, Charlie Frost. Sylvia and I have been divorced for about 10 years. Nothing too upsetting, Sylvia just wanted to trade me in for a younger richer model and I just wanted a quieter life.

I am a writer. Well, to be more accurate, I'm a technical writer. For the most part that means turning in to reasonable English appalling translations of Chinese, Japanese or South Korean instruction pamphlets. I work from home and enjoy being a bit of a recluse. Well I would do except that my ex- mother-in-law, an old bully lives close by still thinks I must do as she says; "You don't vacuum enough! This room is a pigsty! You should shave more often and that shirt, those shoes, your hair, oh! the list was endless.

Well, for a few nights all was well. I made sure I switched off the bedside light and I slept like a top.

It was, I remember, the night of a full moon. I had not drawn the curtains and the shadows on the ceiling were all there. Chimbu was soon at the bottom of my bed.

"Look Charlie, it's time we got down to some serious discussion. You and I are sitting on a gold mine if we co-operate."

To Chimbu 'discussion' means shut up and listen to what I say.

He told me that he had been brought up in America. His master, Blue Foot, was a Sioux Indian and he and Blue Foot were both killed in a skirmish with the Pale Face and had gone to the Happy Hunting Grounds. He said that, after a while, it was boring. He spent his afterlife chasing previously dead Buffalo for happy dead Indians and in the end he had requested a transfer and had eventually finished up on my ceiling.

Over the next few nights he explained his plan. His idea was that I should make it known that I had special powers and would, for a price, re-unite grieving dog lovers with their dear departed pets.

I was, to say the least, nervous of the whole idea and said that I did not feel capable. Chimbu said that by a lucky chance my ex-mother-in-law's odious ancient Pekinese had just died as had the Jack Russell of one of her neighbours and that this gave us an opportunity to set up a practice séance.

Reluctantly, the following morning, I phoned my ex-mother-in-law. She was distraught, Poochy had just died and how did I know. I modestly explained that I had extra-sensory powers and that I would be able to put her in touch with Poochy. She was so upset that she abandoned her usual habit of objecting to everything I did or said and clutched at the idea of a séance and so, one evening, as dusk fell, I found myself in her front room, sitting round a card table, holding hands with my ex-mother-in-law and Alice, her neighbour.

I closed my eyes, took several noisy deep breaths.

"Is there anybody there?" I moaned.

"Look, quit the bloody theatrics and just tell them that Poochy and Jack are anxious to speak to them." Chimbu hissed.

I started again, "I have with me Poochy and Jack and they wish to speak."

I took another noisy deep breath. "Yap, yap, yap yap yap." I could hear Chimbu shouting. "Stop fighting, you'll both get your turn! Bloody Jack Russells are always fighting."

It was chaos. The only sounds from me were yapping and snarling. Alice and my ex-mother-in-law were convinced that they were the victims of a cruel hoax and I was told that they never wished to see me again. Even in this darkest moment I found myself hoping that my ex-mother-in-law would keep to her word.

Chimbu and I met the following night.

"Look! I've got another idea. I've just met a famous dead horse who says his grandson is running tomorrow at Kempton and is a dead cert."

I lost most of my savings when it trailed in last and I am arranging for a decorator to re-do my ceiling.

'Til Death Us Do Part

— ◆ —

"Soon be there, home sweet home" she cooed.

It may be home sweet home to you thought Charles but to me, it's just a prison without bars. Very soon he thought I'll be retired and there'll be no work to escape to.

When Charles and Sue had married nearly forty years ago Sue had been a beautiful gentle wife but as the years had gone by she had become more and more controlling.

"Charles, don't just sit there watching your silly sports program, you know I want you to help me strip the bed and make up the spare room. You know Margaret is coming tomorrow."

Margaret was her sister and her frequent visits ensured that, for a change, the constant stream of commands were in stereo.

"Fetch my slippers from the kitchen Charles and while you're there put the kettle on."

Both of them seemed convinced that Charlie's work on the production line at Ford's was merely rest and that when he came home there they were sitting, waiting for him to start work.

But Charlie's major irritation was chauffeuring Sue, to the shops, to her sisters, a day out, whatever. Sue did not drive but she controlled Charlie's entire world from the passenger seat.

"Don't drive so fast. Don't go that way. Mind that little girl. That's not you're right of way." The commands were incessant.

Worse still these commands were to the accompaniment of loud Radio 2.

Charlie hated it. When he was in the car by himself he loved the serenity of Classic FM but as soon as Sue was in the car she changed to 2 and turned up the volume and at the end of these periods of acute torture she would coo; "Soon be there, home sweet home."

When Sue suddenly died of a massive stoke, Charles, at first felt that his world was empty but as the weeks passed he found the gentle satisfaction of peace. In the car Classic FM soothed all cares and the prospect of retirement, was a joy to be looked forward to. The first minor irritation was the car radio. Of its own accord it would jump from Classic FM to radio 2. Charles got it fixed but then Classic FM reception would break up a little and voices from another program could sometimes be heard. Charles began to think of getting a new car radio or perhaps even a new; more sporty car. One misty evening, as Charlie drove home from his newly discovered, snooker club, the radio reception was at it's worst. He tried re-tuning and then, as clear as if she were sitting next to him, he heard:

"Turn left here, that's it; don't drive too fast it's getting foggy. Take the road toward Cliff Way, I want to look at the sea."

Years of conditioning are impossible to resist. Charles did as he was told.

"Good it's not so foggy here, you don't need to dawdle so. That's it. Faster. Now; TURN LEFT."

As the car lurched off the cliff top Charles heard those final, fatal words:

"Soon be there, home sweet home."

Vagabond

—— ◆ ——

"I travel the road, I follow the stars to .."

The reedy voice was transformed in to electric pulses as the sound engineer tweaked the bass.

"Cut! That's fine Julian we can feed in the library copy for that. All we need is for you to do your 'Good-bye line' and we're finished. When you are ready; go.

"Well all you listeners, thank you and good night. Sleep well but spare a thought for the Vagabond with no bed, just a star to follow." The sound crew busied themselves putting the 20th Vagabond Tales in its place.

"Well done Julian, we do not need to record for a month or so and that will give the writers time to come up with some more rubbish."

"Adrian, I think some of the tales have had a certain resonance. I just wonder at times, if it would be better if to keep the figures high, we leaked to the press my identity."

"We've been over this time and time again Julian! Part of the success is the mystery of who is the vagabond. It would not help if it were known that our secret wandering vagabond was in reality, Julian Meadows living a comfortable existence in West Kensington. Oh! And that reminds me, your driver has phoned in to say that there's been some sort of a delay and he won't be able to pick you up tonight."

Damn thought Julian that means the dear boy is out on the town and I shall be returning to an empty bed. Still perhaps it's all for the best. I feel somehow he's lost his charm. He's, too effeminate. Perhaps I need a change.

As he left the studio Julian paused and considered the weather. A clear starry night sky, rather cold but he turned up the velvet collar of his warm cashmere coat and decided to walk.

The street lights caste his shadow in front of him and he admired the swing of his well tailored, coat. I am wasted in this modern world he thought. I should have been at my best when gentlemen wore silk lined cloaks and shining top hats. I would have really cut a dash.

"Got some change so that I can get a cuppa tea, mate?"

Julian's dear heart missed a beat as he turned to see, huddled in a shop doorway a bundle of clothing.

"You're a fine gentleman! You won't miss a few quid to 'elp a chap 'ose darn on his luck."

Julian's first instincts were to hurry by but something held him there. His eyes adjusted to the gloom of the shadowed doorway.

Hm, quite young, so, so masculine. Dirty, smelly but after a shower; he felt a sexual stirring. Maybe he would join him in the shower.

"Look, I do not carry any money but my apartment is close by. I'll get you a meal, you can have a hot shower and I can probably find some warmer more suitable clothing for you."

George thought, allo! An arse bandit! Better make sure I don't turn my back on 'im.

"Fank you guv'ner. I could do wif a bite to eat and that's for sure. Lead the way."

The apartment was welcoming and warm and the warmth immediately increased the rank smell of George's clothes.

"I say, old chap, why don't you have a nice hot shower while I find you some better clothes and rustle up some food?"

Adrian could hear the sounds of the shower. All that filth disappearing, leaving a young, strong body. It was nearly time for tonight's episode of Vagabond Tales. Perhaps he should switch on the radio. He could imagine themselves sporting on the carpet in front of the fire and him saying, modestly, yes, that's me. I am the Vagabond.

But first I'll join him in the shower.

He slowly opened the bathroom door. In the steam he could see a strong tattooed arm grasping a long back scrubber briskly at work on a handsome back.

He slipped off his toweling dressing gown and entered the shower. "Let me do that for you." He murmured.

George whacked him hard with the wooden scrubber. He hit him again and again.

"I didn't escape from prison and all its poofters to get in to bed with the first queer that offers me a hot meal!" he shouted.

He let the shower wash the blood from himself before stepping out over the lifeless body.

The clothes and coat were an excellent fit, the watch, the money, the quick meal were all acquired.

As he moved to leave the flat, from the radio, he could hear "I travel the road, I follow the stars."

He stopped to listen. He remembered how much he had envied the Vagabond when he had listened in his prison cell.

Nah, he fought, if instead of that old poofter I'd met up wif the Vagabond

Na, that would've been different.

Gladys

— ◆ —

Commander James Bond flung open the door and strode in to the office. He was not in a good mood.

"Morning James," said Moneypenny. "M's been screaming for you for the last hour. You'd better go straight in."

Bond snorted, flung his hat at the hat stand and missed. It was one of those days.

M was no more cheerful.

"007 the government does not pay you a huge amount of tax-payer's money to arrive for a day's work at mid-day. The P.M. expects instant results and you are already 4 hours behind time. You will be on the 1400 hr flight to Cairo. You will be met off the plane and will then be given a full briefing. Moneypenney has all your travel documents and remember, James, there's no time for your perpetual philandering."

James allowed himself another snort when he left M's office. He was beginning to think that, women, M, Moneypenney and the nubile young lady who had shared his bed last night and emptied his wallet before leaving this morning, were too much trouble.

When the plane touched down at Cairo he was in a better mood. Two Airhostesses had pressed their telephone numbers in to his hand with promising prospects.

Q was waiting at customs.

"I've got all your requirements in my car; automatic, watch with all the gadgets. I am happy to say that M has not allowed you to have a car. It seems that budgets have been cut and on almost every mission you undertake, your car is a write-off."

Bond's bad mood returned. He did not know the mission yet, but he did expect a good car chase, usually with a scantily clad girl by his side. He snorted.

"Really Q, don't you lot ever have anything new. You're so predictable!"

"Well it so happens, 007, the we do have this new explosive, so powerful that one gram can punch a hole through inch thick steel." James snorted again but did take a small piece and concealed it behind his watch.

"007, we've booked you in to the Hyatt Hotel and you will be contacted this evening with your briefing. Be there and don't get up to any mischief."

By the evening Bond had ordered a meal in his room, showered and sat sipping a martini wearing just a white toweling dressing gown. There was a gentle tap at the door. 007 concealed his weapon in his dressing gown pocket and slowly opened the door.

He saw a small person clad in a grey burka with just a hint of flashing eyes behind the veil.

"James, it's me, Avril, for god's sake let me in. M sent me."

Inside the room, Avril stripped off the burka, revealing a scantily clad vision.

"God! I'm glad to get out of that. I can't tell you how hot it is. M said I must be discrete so I had to wear that god awful sheet."

She sat on the edge of the bed and from her belt, pulled out a scrap of paper.

Bond sat beside her.

"Before we get down to all that let me pour you a drink. You're so hot, let me loosen that for you."

It was perhaps about 2 in the morning when Avril, demurely clutching a sheet to her bosom, reached for the scrap of paper.

"Look James, will you stop that and let me give you your briefing! Mm, well perhaps it can wait a little longer."

In the morning, when the burka clad Avril had left, James considered his assignment.

When Sheik Omar, the extremist agitator, had been deported from the UK he had settled in a well-fortified estate on the outskirts of Cairo where he continued to spread his gospel of murder via the

Internet. In his double O, licensed to kill role, Bond was instructed to permanently silence the Sheik.

The high wall was topped with bulletproof glass. There was no possibility for a sniper assassination.

Bond phoned Q.

"I want Gladys."

"Oh no," moaned Q, you'll just destroy her."

Gladys arrived the next evening in the care of the ever-enthusiastic Avril and the next morning, Gladys began her training.

For two days Gladys fed only from the white turban, worn for the purpose, by James. On the 3rd day she received no food. James took her to the hill near the estate.

In addition to his message of murder, Sheik Omar preached that birds were Allah's messengers and so, every morning, he arrived on the terrace, to feed the birds.

The hungry Gladys, released by Bond, spied the white turban and headed for food. Like an arrow the pigeon dived over the glass wall and perched on the white turban. 007 pressed the remote detonator. The turban and head disintegrated and of the heroine Gladys, all that was visible was the tail.

Pipe Dream

— ◆ —

He leaned on the fence watching the men working. He had time to spare and the sun, low in the sky, warmed his back increasing his contentment. He remembered how, just 5 years ago, each morning he awoke with a "Tight Chest." He could feel it now but just as a memory.

"John, you must go to the Doctors again. You're not getting any better and I know your not sleeping and you are keeping me awake"

He heard the same thing from Jane every morning. In fact he always went to the Doctor with same opening joke; "I've got this noise in my ears Doctor. It's my wife constantly telling me to come and see you."

He did not need to go to the Doctor to know what was wrong. There was nothing the GP could do unless he could get him a new job.

He had started work at Latimers, straight from school, nearly 30 years ago. He had always been ambitious, hardworking. He enjoyed the challenges and rewards of promotion. He married Joan, had a dog and a large mortgage and faced the future with the calm expectation of increasing unchecked security.

It had all started to go wrong just 5 years ago when old Saunders had retired. John had confidently expected to take over and steer the company to new heights but without explanation the directors appointed an outsider.

Young Charles Miller had a university degree and little else as far as John was concerned. It bit into his soul to think that the ever expanding organization that was in a great part due to his efforts was given to a young know all with a piece of paper and a plumy accent.

"Call me Charles. I am going to need all the help I can get from you," he said with a false modest smile. John had gritted his teeth and realized that he had no alternative but to make the best of it. He had no other skills to take to a new company. He was over the hill and had to accept it.

But he could not. He found the decisions were made without reference to him. Promotions were made that offended his self-esteem and as if to rub salt into his bleeding wounds Joan, his wife, began to treat him with contempt.

"Why has young Ericson been sent on the course and not you?"

"You should not have to stay late to recast the balances, that's a junior's job."

"Can't we, just for once afford a GOOD holiday?"

He developed a "Chest." He had, on occasions to take time off sick. He wheezed at night. As time past he saw himself as no more than a timeserving worm slowly crawling toward retirement.

There was talk of a take-over or, as Mr Miller called, "A merger."

Mr Charles Miller sent for him. Miller had, over the years developed a smug sense of his own importance. There were grave words about reorganizations, economies, unpleasant decisions. The platitudes droned on but what John heard was; "You are not wanted. At 50 you are on the scrap heap. He forced himself to listen;

"Generous redundancy package, pension rights at 60. He cleared his desk and left.

John did not want to go home but there was nowhere else to go. She had cried;

"What will I do? What will the neighbors say? Oh the shame."

John found no comfort. Jane had decreed that no one must know. It was to be a shameful secret. He felt he must have some disease that polite people never spoke about. He continued to wheeze.

He found peace on Sunday mornings. They got up late, Jane went to church with a coffee meeting to follow, John had a peaceful house and a heavy paper to read.

"Would you like to be the master of your fate? Would you like to be your own boss?" The words leapt out to him. It was an advertisement at the side of an article on Franchising." It set off within him a dream. Yes he would. He could see himself "Master"

"A success" "His own boss" "Respected." There was a telephone number. It said to phone anytime. He did. He arranged an appointment for the following Wednesday. He did not tell Jane.

The appointment was at a local hotel and he was unhappy to find that there were several men there, carbon copies of himself.

There was a video about landscape gardening and then two well-dressed, confident young men spoke of enormous sums of money. For just a modest capital investment there was a fortune to be made. John heard the man next to him mutter,

"I thought they would want our money."

All of the men left when the formal proceedings were finished with words like;

"Have to think about it."

But John stayed on. It would take a large slice of his redundancy money to buy the equipment from them and he would need to buy a small pick-up truck as they had suggested. They would provide back up, learning courses, design work, supplies and extensive advertising. John signed all the forms.

He calculated that after all the expenditures he would have enough money to survive a year.

He did not tell Jane. He knew she would be against it;

"What will the neighbors say?"

"Risking our money."

"What if it goes wrong? What about me?"

On Friday he ordered a little green pick-up and on the Sunday, just before she was going to work he told Jane his plans. She cried.

"What about me?" she said? "What will the neighbors say?"

She did not go to church as John had hoped. She stayed to give John the benefit of incessant lectures on the need to look after her, on the frauds of franchising, on how she could not endure the shame of having an odd job man as a husband and finally on the dangers of early senility. John began to wheeze. Retired to bed. The doctor was called.

On the following Friday John went to collect his pickup. They had not been able to get a green one but had managed, at such short notice to get a bright red one. John loved it. As agreed they took his neat saloon in part exchange.

He gave it a little test drive through the town and then drove home and parked it outside the house.

Jane packed and left to live with her widowed sister. That was 5 years ago.

"Come on lads, it's time to knock off. You can get it finished tomorrow."

He chatted to them for a few minutes. Phillip, the youngest of them, admired John's new shining car.

"I tell you what," said John, "You can drive me home."

As they approached the town center he saw Charles Miller. He was just leaving the library. He looked older, smaller, anxious and shabby. John had read recently that they company had closed and he presumed that Miller, along with all the others, was now redundant.

"I wonder how it would be if I gave him a job," thought John.

A Stag Chases a Doe Until...

— ◆ —

All the young stags agreed that Ata was very desirable. "Look at those eyes," said one. Another said, "I'd like to give that rump a going over." As spring began to stir their blood their comments became more lustful.

But Hip said nothing. He hung back from the other stags so as to worship from afar. He loved Ata and had done since he had first seen her skipping and jumping, floating and flying above the ground in the meadow. All the other does ran with flailing hooves pounding the turf. Ata floated like a gentle breeze just stirring the grass.

It was Melly who made the first move. With a throaty roar he advanced. Ata turned and ran. Melly was not surprised. All Does run at first, the thrill of the chase makes capture and conquest more exciting. He began to gain on her but instead of slowing after the token reluctance, Ata lifted her heels and moved ahead. Melly was irritated. Now this was not a matter of lust this was a contest of honour. No Doe can outrun a fit young stag. Ata played him disdainfully. When Melly thundered toward her she would slow and then like a Matador playing a Bull, she would float just out of reach. In despair he charged blindly into a thicket entangling his antlers from which he was unable to extricate himself and endured a lingering death.

Alcar fared no better. He chased Ata far away over the hills. She returned in the evening but Alcar was never seen again.

Hip knew he could not outrace her. He was so ordinary and she was a goddess. One evening he consulted Aphro. She was the oldest and the wisest of the Does.

"What am I going to do Aphro? She's so wonderful and I'm so ordinary?"

Aphro resisted the impulse to say that Ata was no different to the others. Instead she said;

"Well I know she's very partial to a nice ripe apple. Why don't you try getting some and when you race, drop an apple so that she stops to eat it. I think if you do this two or three times you'd probably catch her."

Hip stole the apples from a parked lorry. They were "Golden Delicious."

He carried them carefully in his mouth and decided that he would make his move the following day.

But Hip spent a restless night. He knew the trick would probably work but it seemed so unsporting. He awoke with the thought that he would and could not cheat. Leaving the apples he wandered away from the others preferring his own sad company.

Ahead of him, bathed in golden sunlight, he saw his love. She was alone.

Ata seemed unaware of him and he approached quietly. It's now or never, he thought. He lifted his head to give a mighty roar but what emerged sounded like an apologetic cough.

Ata reacted. She turned away and began to run. Hip was in full pursuit. He was gaining on her. Perhaps he noticed her limping but, by now, his thoughts of fair play were overwhelmed by his desire. Ata turned into the woods, stopped and turned to face him. Her nostrils were flared and she was panting hard. She limped towards him and playfully nipped his neck. As their steaming flanks touched he could feel her racing heart beating beside his.

That night, while Hip slept in deep contentment, Ata limped to a pool.

"Stags are such simple creatures," she thought.

"I have loved Hip since I first saw him that day in the meadow. There he was, standing so aloof, so handsome, like a prince. I thought he would never chase such an ordinary Doe as me."

She hummed contentedly as she dipped her hooves in to the pool to wash out the pebbles she had put there that morning.

Time for a Holiday

—◆—

Mrs. Jeffreys looked at the card that had plopped through her letterbox that morning. No name or address just the bold statement that a simple phone call would be all that was necessary to obtain free valuations of old furniture and jewelry. Just what she needed! Quite a well-spoken voice had answered the mobile phone number. Mrs. Jeffreys had explained that she was reluctantly thinking of selling some of her possessions and the kindly voice had agreed to call.

She decided that, when he came, she would offer to make tea and his tea would be in the Edward 6th coronation mug.

Charlie Walker looked at the house. Neat, semi, nothing remarkable still, as his dad always said, "You can't tell a book by its cover." He rang the bell.

A quavering voice called out, "Just a minute," and he heard slow shuffling steps. She looked frail with wispy grey hair. She peered anxiously round the edge of the door.

"Mrs. Jeffreys? My name's Walker, Charles Walker, you called me about a valuation."

"Did I? Oh, silly me! Of course I did. I'll be forgetting my own name soon. Yes, you'd better come in."

She shuffled her way ahead of him, in to a small sitting room.

Already Charlie could see that Mrs. Jeffreys' house was a receptacle for the bizarre. Behind the front door was a large stuffed bear that seemed to act as an umbrella stand. In the sitting room every flat surface was covered with; well, everything and every vertical surface was festooned with pictures, clocks, posters and plates. On the small sideboard was a man's opera hat that contained a plant pot of faded paper flowers. At first glance Charlie could see almost everything in the room was rubbish but then he saw her.

She was an oil painting, not too large, just a tastefully draped, full-length nude. He remembered his dad's advice. "Don't show interest in what's good, stick to the rubbish," but her eyes seemed to follow him across the room.

The old lady was telling him that some of the wall clocks were old and perhaps of value. Charlie could see they were of little real value.

"Look!" she said, "I'll make you a nice mug of tea while you have a look around."

She shuffled off to the kitchen and he hurried across to the picture. Yes, it was signed, perhaps it needed a little cleaning but it was an early Phillip Preston, very collectable. Should fetch £20,000 to £30,000 maybe more.

Mrs. Jeffreys busied herself in the kitchen but was well able to see, through the half-shut door, the young man's careful scrutiny.

She thought to herself of the time when she, as a young nurse at the Royal Infirmary, had posed naked for Philip, an impoverished painter and how so many sittings had been terminated by passion. That picture was the shining memory of her life's love. The kettle boiled.

Mr. Walker was carefully examining one of the clocks when she came back with the tea. She could see that he had noticed the mug. Charlie, sipped his tea, examined the marks on some of the plates and shook his head.

"Well Mrs. Jeffreys, you've got some nice stuff here but there's not much of a market for it and it would be near robbery to deprive you of your precious knick-knacks."

"Oh! Don't say that Mr. Walker. I've got bills to pay. I did so hope that you would be able to help me. Surely some of those clocks must be worth something."

"Well, I suppose one might be worth £50 or so but that don't go very far these days."

It seemed that Mrs. Jeffreys was near to tears. "What shall I do?" Charlie hesitated. Now was the time to make the killing. He could see himself, next visiting day, telling his father of the small fortune he had made.

"Well, I've taken quite a fancy to that little painting you've got there. It looks like quite a good copy and I wouldn't mind it myself.

I tell you what I'll do. I'll give you £500 pound for the clock, this mug, which you won't need to wash and that picture. How would that suit?"

"Mrs. Jeffreys sobbed. I haven't got the money for the house. The gas bills final notice. My lovely picture!"

She shook her head, sobbed again and Charlie was surprised to find that, for the addition of one more clock and the opera hat he had committed himself to £2,000.

She would not take a cheque. Her husband, God rest his soul, had warned her "Only cash is king."

Charlie left in a hurry. He could just get to the bank in time.

When he returned Mrs. Jeffreys had taken down the clocks and the painting and washed the mug. She carefully counted the money and seemed to hug a fond farewell to her painting as, wrapped in an old blanket, he put it in the van.

When the van had gone Mrs. Jeffreys walked briskly back in to the house.

He deserves whatever he gets she thought, telling me that the picture was a nice copy. Well. I've only got two more copies but I've got the real one to put back on my wall.

Bees Behaving Badly

———— ◆ ————

Hi! My name's Buzz but then, we are all called Buzz. We are all workers and as far as the commune is concerned we are all equal it's just that some of us are more equal than others and I always had the ambition to be the most equal.

Take for example Buzz. When our hive was moved to the West Country Buzz soon became the most successful worker in the hive. Because we were in a new area it was necessary for all the workers to survey the surrounding countryside to find the best sources of nectar and pollen and each evening, Buzz came back with information on new, fantastic sources.

Now there is a stupid tradition in Beehives for the most successful find to be celebrated, after supper, with a game called, "Dancing Charades." The bee that has the best information starts a sort of dance and all the rest of us have to guess from dance where the new, super-source was located. Well, Buzz came back almost every day with news like a fantastic field of lavender or apple- blossom and all I seemed to find were fields of Oil Seed Rape and that makes terrible honey. I said to my friend Buzz, no not that one, another one, that I never got the chance to do the dance. I got so that my work fell off. I would leave the hive in the morning and just sort of wander around sometimes practising a little dance of my own and just buzzing, "I want my chance to do the dance."

Now this day I found nothing. It was a late summer's evening and I had no nectar, no pollen. I was tired and thirsty so I rested up at a small cottage. There was a little old lady dressed for bed, making herself a cup of chocolate. When she had drunk it she left the mug with the dregs, beside the sink and went to bed.

Well, as I said, I was thirsty so I buzzed up to the mug, stuck in my proboscis and slurped up some cool cocoa.

Man, it was cool, I mean, man, it was like cool. I took another slurp. Swinging man! Like flying without moving. Like my head was buzzing without buzzing. Man it was cool, I mean cool. I tried to fly home but my left wings seemed weak and I just moved in small circles, dizzy man. I jived back to the windowsill and settled for the night.

In the morning I woke when the lady came in the kitchen to make breakfast.

She made a bowl of cereal and added a teaspoonful of what looked like tea leaves.

I had my breakfast from the residues.

Man oh man! Same hit, same buzzing, man, I'm spaced out!

I think I floated back to the windowsill.

I got my wings back about mid-day and I buzzed in to the garden where the old lady was working, watering some strange looking plants. No flowers, no nectar. She picked off a few leaves and laid them in the sun to dry. I nibbled a leaf and fell to the ground. Man! I was zonked, I mean, spaced out, I mean, wicked!

I woke at sunset and headed back to the hive just in time to see Buzz, yeah, the one, starting his stupid dance. I landed on the dance area and pushed him off. Man, I did some dance! All the Buzzes were trying to guess. No, there's no nectar, no, no pollen nor flowers. Just leaves!

"Aw, come on Buzz," they said, "Next you'll be telling us, it's a field of grass!"

The conservative, more died in the wool, were too skeptical but I did find one or two including Buzz, yea my one, who agreed to come with me in the morning.

The rest is history. Man, we had a ball and did not get back to the hive for three days but when we did, we jived man, we jived.

From that day on, half the work force, under my direction, collected leaves from the cottage. The other half collected the usual nectar and back at the hive, we added a little dried leaf to all the stored honey.

Honey sales rocketed as more and more people learned of the new, "Hot Honey," –For that extra buzz. There was a time when we hit supply problems when the old lady was detained at her majesty's pleasure but she's out now and we are increasing production.

Some say that the leaf will affect our brains, but I don't see it. I mean, we only get it for our personal use and The Queen is considering passing a new law to legalise moderate usage. I mean man, way out man. I mean man, I'm now head buzz man and I dance and jive whenever I like man.

The God Father

———— ◆ ————

I am sure, George my stepfather, just married my mother for her money. I mean, she's 50 and well past her sell by date but, whatever, my mum married him last year and I not only got George but two odious step brothers. And me? Well I'm just left out in the cold. Take this week for instance, mum, George Henry and Richard have gone off on holiday to Florida but I'm not allowed to go 'cos' someone has to look after Button. Button is the family dog and I quite like him but I'd rather be in Florida.

Oh, I'm John Julian Smith aged 20, single, no girl friend and a trainee horologist, which makes me very uninteresting.

The phone rings.

"Is that you J J? This is Jules. How are you?"

Jules is an old university chum of my mother. My real dad used to tease her about Jules. Said that he was only her friend because she felt safe with him because he only liked men. But, whatever, he and Mum were close and when I was born, Mum insisted that he be my Godfather. He takes his duties very seriously.

I tell Jules how they've all gone of on holiday and how I'm pretty miffed having to look after Button.

"Dear Boy," he says, "You shall have a holiday. I'm supposed to be going to a festival in Vienna but I've broken my ankle and can't go. Everything is arranged, you can take my place and I will look after Button."

Julian is something big in government, in Arts and Culture. I tell him how lovely that would be but that I don't have all the right clothes.

"Nonsense, dear boy. We are about the same size, I'll fit you out and I am sure you will look the part. You can go as my personal representative. All expenses paid. You fly to Vienna and while you are there you'll have a government car. Now, J J how does that sound to you? You'd have a super time and will be doing me a big favour."

What could I say but yes. There would be a week of Opera, Ballet and Concerts starting with a Ball at the Opera House.

I look fantastic in Julian's clothes. He's a bit flamboyant, with lacy cuffs on silk shirts and the black tie and tails are beautifully cut to show off a trim waist and broad shoulders and I have the pick of his wardrobe. I feel like a new man. The clothes make me feel taller, smarter, more interesting.

A limo' takes me to the airport, first-class flight and a limo' meets me at the airport. I am staying at the British Ambassador's residence and am waited on like royalty.

At the ball the Ambassador, Sir Geoffrey Lyons, "Call me Geoff," and his wife, Lady Cynthia, "Call me Cyn," introduce me as J J, representative of her majesty's Government for Arts and Culture. So much colour! So many beautiful people! So many famous names and then, across a crowded room I became aware of a pair of deep blue eyes, golden hair exquisite figure, regal bearing. I am introduced. It is love at first sight for me and for Sissy, French Attaché for Cultural Affairs.

Now, I live in Paris with Sissy and he and I agree that we owe so much to my Fairy Godfather.

The Other Man

—— ◆ ——

There is a knock at the door and Tserlina runs down stairs to open it. She studies the 30 something man standing there. He is wearing an excellent well-cut suit, tall, dark with a slim moustache.

"Good morning young lady, my name is Rossi and I am here, by appointment to view the house. You are, I hope, expecting me?"

"Well yes," she says "But my Mother is out for the next hour or two and I don't know if I can be of much help but you can come in if you wish to."

He enters and casts a professional eye around the small hall.

"Hm, this will need altering and this I presume is your 'Front Room'"

He hurries through the sitting room, purses his lips at the state of the kitchen.

"It's all a bit of a mess today I'm afraid because I'm getting married at 4 o'clock this afternoon and my Mum and Sister have both dashed off to get their hair done."

"And, you are the bride and you do not need to get your hair done? No you don't it is already perfectly charming. And, will you be married in that dress?"

Tserlina blushes as she straightens the errant hem line of her skirt.

"No no, my dress is upstairs and there is plenty of time before I have to get ready."

"And who is the man who will this day win such a beautiful jewel as you?"

"Oh! er, Charlie Brooks. We've been going out for over 6 months."

"And what does this Mr Charlie Brooks do? How will he care for such perfection as you?"

"My Charlie is doing well and he has good prospects. He's a trainee butcher and soon he will be managing his own shop with a lovely flat above it for our very own."

"For your very own. A flat above a butchers. Such beauty as yours should not be allowed to flower in a flat above a shop of dead meat. If you were mine I would find the perfect setting to allow your beauty to be seen and worshiped. I already have at least a 100 house like this and blocks of flats, enough money to last many life times but more than that, if you were mine, I would cherish you, love you so that we would experience pleasures that no oaf of a trainee butcher could ever achieve. We would.

"My Charlie's not an Oaf he's, he's.."

"Well what is he? I can give you the world and what is your name?

"Tserlina."

"Tserlina, a beautiful name to grace a goddess. Tell me beautiful Tserlina, do you have a passport?"

"Yes I have we are going today, after my wedding to Majorca for a weeks honeymoon."

"And I have a yacht with a small crew in harbour not an hour from here. In just one hour we could be setting sail to anywhere. To the Greek Islands or the Caribbean Sea or where our flights of fancy take us. We can lie under the stars and let our bodies melt in to one. We can experience passion to lift us above the stars, nights of unending passion."

"I can't. I don't even know your name. I can't. What could I tell Charlie?"

"Tell him nothing. Come Tserlina get your passport; leave a note for your Mother she can deal with the oaf. Come my beautiful Tserliana come with me Giovanni let us waste no more time. Let us go.

"Yes Giovanni let's go.

Phant and Co.

—— ◆ ——

"Hrrmp, ah Miss Ella, will you pass the word along the line to young Sicko, I want a word with him at the double. Ah! Young Sicko, jump in, don't stand on ceremony, there's plenty of room, that's the way; there's no need to be shy young fella-me-lad, here, have some mud."

"Oh thank you Colonel, this is such a great honour. Would it be all right if I moved a little to the other side? I do so admire your tusks. They look so wonderful gleaming in the sunlight. I do so feel…"

"Hrrmp! Yes, well young fella, I did not invite you to my mud hole to admire my tusks. I want a few words with you and I don't want to beat about the bush, so to speak. I flatter myself that I know how to come straight to the point. Although I do feel that you show remarkable taste in admiring these old tusks. They are, of course rather battered nowadays. It hasn't always been easy to manage Fant Company. In the past we have been in some tight situations. Did I ever tell you of the time when, with only Miss Ella for support, I captured three, very desirable young cows from under the trunk of General Derm? It was, as I remember, at the mud hole just by the shinning river. What a time that was! I remember how…"

"Oh yes Colonel sir. I do so love to hear you tell that story how the

General was so exhausted from his efforts with Miss Patty Derm, that he couldn't even raise a tusk to give chase."

Hrrmp! Well this won't do. We must stick to the point. Now, what was it I wanted to say? Ah yes! Young Sicko I have been very impressed by your foraging work and have had high hopes that, one day, if you kept your trunk to the grindstone, in the distant future, when I must hand over to younger blood, that you would take up the challenge."

"Oh thank you Colonel sir, I am sure that that day is far away and even then, I do not feel that there is one elephant anywhere who could hold a tusk to you."

"Hrrmp! What I want to say, young Sicko, I've been getting complaints from the young cows about your behaviour. Why, only yesterday I saw you in the mud pool with Miss Toothsome Fant and I could not help but observe, how shall I put this? Yes! I could not help but observe that you were displaying a fifth leg. Mister Sicko Fant, I will not have any young Bull staying in My preserves.".

"Colonel sir, that was just morning stiffness. I would not presume to make such advance."

"Hrrmp! Well, be that as it may, I have also had a serious complaint from Miss Sylvia Balls, who says that yesterday, while we were on morning patrol, you approached from the rear and placed both your tusk and trunk in a very tender area. She was shocked."

"Colonel, sir, that was an accident. We were in single file and I did not hear your call to halt and I continued when Miss Sylvia had come to a stop.

"It's no good young Sicko, I will not allow sexual harassment. I am going to have to let you go but before you go, let me give you a few words of advice. There is a whole world out there for you to make your mark in but be very careful, it's a jungle where, dog eats dog and you can trust no one. Now, Mister Sicko Fant, listen carefully. I have decided to give you a helping hand. I am going to let you have Miss Ella. She is rather long in the tusk but has done excellent service in the past and I am sure there are still several gallons left in her tank.

I must also inform you that just south of here, is a small watering hole where I have observed two unattached young cows one of whom has enchanting wrinkled legs and the other is huge. When she walks by the earth moves."

"Oh thank you Colonel sir, south you said?"

"Hrrmp, yes, I said south and that is why you will be going north. Later today, I intend to lead the troop south, on a mission of mercy and I do not want you within fifty miles of them so, pack your trunk, take Miss Ella and go north young Sicko."

Black Box

◆

Professor Lee Porter looked around the small selected audience assembled in the lecture theatre. This was, he thought, his moment of glory, his pathway to a peerage, his election to the Royal Society and yes, perhaps the Nobel Prize. His heart skipped a beat, the formalities were completed and he moved to the lectern.

"Ladies and gentlemen, distinguished guests, friends. Thank you for coming to share with me what I hope to be a momentous occasion."

The large viewing monitor glowed as he pressed a button and in the center of the screen appeared a box.

"This box is taken from an aircraft. It is 'The Black Box" that records all the vital functions of an aircraft in flight and as you well know, is extremely significant in the event of a flying catastrophe It was this thought that led me to consider the infinite value of such a device in relation to the living human body. What if a miniaturized 'Black Box' could be fitted in a human body and connected to the brain and other vital organs? What data could we find when that living body crashed?"

The Professor was not prepared to let his moment of glory be brief and he droned on and on about miniaturization, medical ethics, costs, but the upshot of it all was that he had implanted such a box in the abdominal cavity of a terminally ill male patient who had now died and the box recovered.

He explained that that the box was now connected to the computer and that they were together, to witness the thoughts of the subject at time of death and perhaps beyond. He expanded at length about near death experiences where patients had, on recovery recounted tales of them leaving their bodies and moving toward a bright light only to be recalled.

At this point the Professor of Divinity asked the Professor a question.

"No my Lord, I agreed with the patient that I would only review the material near the actual time of death although the recordings should exist from the moment the device was implanted. We should hear those thoughts, converted by the computer in to speech although it may be that the quality of speech may be rather robotic."

Finally, the professor started the recordings after explaining that he would have to sample the tape for some moments to arrive at the point of death.

"Pompous little arse, just 'cos he's got a stethoscope."

The metallic voice rang out perhaps a little too loud.

"No that's not it, I'll fast forward."

"Bloody bed pan! No wonder I'm consti.."

"Further forward I think."

"Nice boobs."

"Further on."

"Stupid fool said I only had a week or so and yet I'm still here a month later."

"Nearly there. That's it. Twenty second of August, nine fifteen."

This was it. The lecture room fell silent.

"I feel like I need a bottle. I think I'm going to wet the bed. I can see.."

Even the robotic voice could not conceal its rising excitement.

"I can see a bright light and now I can.."

The screen flickered and then a message appeared.

'Memory Stick Needs Replacing'

Extinction

— ◆ —

I had got in to the habit of dropping in to the Pub on my way home from work. Most days there were just one or two regulars and I would nod, "G'd evening" and settle to my first pint on a stool in my little corner by the bar but one evening, I was rather annoyed to see a perfect stranger already sitting in My seat.

"G'd evening" I said, ordering my pint, feeling lost without my usual corner. He nodded a reply.

I drank my pint too quickly. It's not the same without your own seat.

"Can I tempt you to another?" he said and signalled to the barman for two more pints.

"Thanks," I said and pulled up a stool beside him.

"Haven't seen you before." I chatted.

"No, I'm not from round here."

"On business?" I asked. I'm polite you see. If a stranger wants to buy me a drink then I am prepared to make conversation.

"Not really" he said. "You see I've just made £10 million and I don't know what to do with it. I spose I'm in a bit of a daze."

"Well" I said, every week I dream of winning the lotto and if I won, I'd be off to somewhere warm and exotic like a shot. Any way, what happened, did you win the lottery?"

"No! Look, let's sit over there at that table. I need to talk to someone and it better be someone who don't know me."

We sat, face to face, across the small table.

"Go on." I urged, "What happened?" Perhaps, I thought, a chap that's got £10 million might drop some of it in my direction.

"Well," he said, "I work, I mean I worked in the research department of Exeter Domestic Products. I'm sure you've heard of them. Well, we were trying to formulate a new spray for wiping food work top surfaces. You know, 'Kills 99% of all know germs' well we wanted something more effective. We'd already got a slogan for the product, 'Kills 110% of all know and unknown germs.' We'd decided to call it, 'Exeter's Extermination Surface Wipe' We'd worked for months trying different formulations but none were quite right. The best one, with one wipe over a Formica surface would make it totally sterile but unfortunately it also wiped away the Formica surface.

He paused to take a long drink from his pint.

"Go on," I said, "But what's that got to do with £10 million?

He wiped his lips with his sleeve and continued.

"Well, I took some of the stuff home and did some experiments of my own. I tried out different dilutions and solvents and discovered that one drop diluted in 1,000 gallons of water was lethal."

"What d'you mean, lethal?" I asked.

"Well it kills everything; germs, fish, dogs, rats, you name it, it kills it."

"What about human beings? Doesn't it kill them?

"Well, of course I didn't try it on humans. My wife was very upset when the dog died but I didn't tell her how. I did not tell anyone at the company. I just handed in my notice and left."

He began to whisper, "I made some enquiries and sold the formula, on the quiet, to the CIA for £2million. Seems they wanted it for defensive work. Then I thought, if they want it for £2 million, perhaps the Russians would like to buy it. I got £4 million from them and then, last week I sold it to the Iraqi chap, Saddam Hussain, got £4 million from him."

"But isn't this all dangerous!" I said, "They'll all be infecting our water supplies and we'll all be dead!"

"No" he whispered, "Stands to reason doesn't it? They've all got it so none of them will dare use it."

We sat there in silence, thinking.

I watched a chap come in and order a double whisky. It looks like he needs that, I thought. He took a long drink, neat and then added a splash of water from the jug on the bar.

"I can't bear to think about it." I said. "Some idiots going to use it and we'll all be goners."

"No," he said, "Stands to reason, nobody would be that stupid."

The fellow at the bar drained the last of his whisky and fell to the floor.

"I do hope he's drunk," I said.

The Ball Was Out

———— ◆ ————

The editor called me in, "Look John," he said, "The owner of Safe Eating Guide wants us to do an article on some fish farm at Little Wittering. Here's the number, contact them and get back to me with a thousand or so words, not too anti GM. Oh, and take a camera." I looked up Little Wittering. It's near Farnham in Surrey so I was able to leave Putney at a reasonable hour the next day to drive to Little Wittering for a 10 o'clock appointment.

I arrived in the village about half an hour early. 'Little' challenges the trade descriptions act. 'Minute' Wittering would be more accurate. A few pretty cottages, no pub, no shop, dilapidated church, three modern looking barns and a tennis court. The largest of the three barns held the sign, "Feed The World Ltd."

I waited in my car until nearer the time I was expected. A man in a white coat was waiting at the door below the sign. He held out his hand.

"You must be Mr. John Sunnucks from Safe Eating. I'm Doctor Fredericks but everyone calls me Fred. Come in."

The door led into a small office with desk, chair and little else. He hesitated.

"Look, very many of the projects we undertake are strictly government secrets but we are close to a breakthrough with one of our projects and that, I have permission to show you. We will of course, need sight of any article before it goes to print but I'm sure that will be no problem."

I nodded and with a flourish, he flung open the door and indicated for me to enter.

I don't know what I was expecting but I certainly was expecting more than a large gloomy interior lined with small fish tanks, all full of bubbling water and nothing else that I could see.

He gestured toward them, "These are merely the nursery tanks. What you are here to meet is Miranda."

We passed through into another room where there was just one larger tank. It was just filled with water enough to cover the one occupant that appeared to be an octopus."

"Miranda," he pronounced, "Is the future of world food production."

I obviously did not seem too impressed. I could not imagine anyone happily eating any part of loathsome Miranda.

"You may think that Miranda is just an octopus but no, Miranda is the product of my personal four year transgenic project."

I looked round for a chair. Years of experience has led me to know that I was about to have my ears assailed by a long winded incomprehensible scientific gobble de goop.

I tried to interject questions like; "Is Miranda GM" but nothing stopped him.

It seems that the original octopus embryonic cell had put in it a newt gene for rapid regenerative properties, a string of salmon genes for high protein meat and a secret gene he was not prepared to identify that gave Miranda smooth tentacles and thin skin.

I think it took him at least an hour to impart this information and I was feeling that without a chair I had reached the limit of my attention span but I give him credit, he caught my complete attention with his final demonstration.

He pulled a table in front of the tank and rang a bell. Immediately Miranda pushed two tentacles out of the tank and waved them in the air. He shook golden breadcrumbs on the table and rang the bell again. Miranda lowered the tentacles and rolled them in the crumb on the table and then Dr Fredricks took a cleaver and with one blow cut off both tentacles. They lay, still writhing, on the table.

"There you are" he said, "These can be chopped in to 4 inch lengths, squared up and deep frozen. Perfect, high protein, fish fingers. Would you like to try some?"

I managed to shake my head and he carried on explaining that Miranda would regenerate the two tentacles in 4 days so she was able to supply two a day. He enthused of the day when thousands of cloned Mirandas would be in production to feed the starving masses and no, Miranda was not GM she was transgenic, that is genes from other species.

I could not get out quick enough.

I felt I had returned from some strange new world to rural England. Two young ladies were playing tennis. A donkey was feeding on the uncut grass protected by the netting around the court and all was right with world. I did not want to linger long but the sight of those two girls in healthy activity eased my mind. I paused. The tall blonde, with effortless grace, leaped to smash the ball passed the despairing racket of the shorter, curvier brunette.

"Out " she shouted.

"You can't be serious. That ball was on the line." Said the donkey.

The Beach Hut

—— ◆ ——

For a moment the sun broke through the clouds flecking the waves with silver and turning the beach to gold. William Clark felt his gloom lighten and decided to make himself a cup of tea. He found a tea bag and powdered milk in the cupboard. His fingers shook as he tried to light the gas ring. "I must remember to buy some more tea bags" he muttered and then stopped himself as he remembered he would never be there again.

Easing himself into the deck chair he sat nursing the hot mug and listened to the waves lapping the shore. No one could see him in the hut but he could hear the laughter of children playing on the beach. "Don't go too near the water Jenny don't you dare get those clothes wet as well"

They had bought the beach hut about 20 years ago when he was 50. He and his wife, May had spent most of their days here watching the waves and listening to the children. Their only child had died when she was 6 years old and, as the years had passed and the pain eased, they had found that the hut gave them the chance to enjoy from a distance, other peoples' children. They had seen in all those childrens' faces their own "Dear Alice" They fretted if they saw a child stray and relaxed only when the child was returned to safety. May had been killed two years ago in a road accident. He had fancied a "Little bit of fish for his supper" and May had slipped on her coat and hurried to the shops. He had heard the squeal of brakes, the thud and the silence, which followed. At the door he could see May, lying still, in the road. Just beyond her outstretched hand was the newspaper package with his "Little bit of fish."

At first William had felt lost, empty. Purposeless but this summer, he had taken to coming back to the hut and to take comfort from watching the children at play.

Last night, as he was preparing to go to bed, he heard a noise. He peered around the curtain and had been stunned as the window shattered beside him. He could hear angry shouting. William felt that his knees would not hold him and he crouched on the floor, hugging his knees to his chest and cried. He cried for himself, for May and "Dear Alice". Why couldn't they leave him alone? Why must they hate him? He seemed to hear May saying; "Don't cry Billy love. It'll be alright."

William Clark finished his tea and stood up. He could see around the door and there, on the beach were the children playing. Just like last week. He forced himself to recall what had happened.

He had been watching the children and had seen one toddler detach from the group and head, un-noticed toward the sea. Suddenly a wave had bowled her over and deposited her, face down, in the sand. He did not think. He acted. He hurried to pick her up. She was crying and he tried to brush the sand from her face and body. She began to scream and wriggle. He clasped her more tightly for fear that she may fall and hurt herself. He tried to pat her, to soothe her. She screamed again.

116

But now there was a crowd, a hostile crowd. "Leave her alone you dirty old man! Voices were coming from all sides. "I was just trying to help," he said. No-one heard him. As the crowd grew so did the noise of self-righteous indignation. One woman snatched the child from him and the child's screams rose to a crescendo. A portly young man saw his moment of glory and seized the dangerous paedophiliac in an imagined vice like grip. "I've got him," he said, "Somebody fetch the police."

William Clark locked the door and walked away. He felt May's arm around him and the warmth of "Dear Alice's hand in his own

The Theagull

—— ◆ ——

It ith not eathy being a theagull if you have a thlight thpeech impediment. All the other theagulls laugh at me because I can't thwark or thweech. I like to keep mythelf to mythelf. I wish I could be an albertroth and follow a lonely thip acroth the theven theas but I have not got the thamina. I have to do the beth I can. I follow the croth channel ferry.

In the small cabin Hetty, gently brushed the hair from Bunty's tear stained, red puffed cheeks. Bunty put her thumb in her mouth and snuggled down. At last, sighed Hetty, she's asleep.

Hetty could hear the creaking noise from the car deck below and the constant throb of the engines and yet, it all seemed so silent. She looked at her watch. It was nearly mid-night. She thought about the past week, now she could see, it had not been a good idea for her and Bunty to have joined the other wives and girl friends on the tour week in France. Standing in the cold, watching fifteen grown men, representing an obscure English rugby club, hurl themselves against fifteen Frenchmen in a sea of mud was no holiday. Three such occasions in one week was three too many.

Far worse, was the intervening times which seemed to be spent incessantly in dark, noisy bars where the wives would huddle

118

together in one corner, trying not to notice the juvenile antics of their drunken partners.

Perhaps, thought Hetty, I could slip out quietly and try to find John. I do not want him bursting in here and waking Bunty when I have just managed to get her to sleep. She tiptoed out, quietly closing the door behind her

There were no wives left in the bar, just the usual raucous singing from the louts at the bar but no John. She waited in case John would return but he did not. Perhaps he had gone up on deck to sober up.

Thith is not a night to be out, I thought. No moon, juth a cold dark drithle. I wath flying high and the deck looked beautiful, silent, empty, with thrings of lighth thparkling in the wet. Behind the thip, below me, the white wake threamed acroth the dark thea.

I thwooped down to reth on the thern. I could now thee that the cold deck wath not detherted. Thaggering towarth the bow wath a young man. In that thate, I thought, he thould not be alone on the deck. I flew towardth him and followed him to the bow. He was thinging. He climbed up on to the rail, leaned forward and thretched out hith armth.

What a thilly man, I thought. He could fall over. I with thomeone would come to thop him!

Hetty looked out on to the deck. There he was, acting like an idiot! She could hear him singing. This is not the Titanic, she thought and you are no DeCaprio. She ran toward him, her soft shoes making no noise on the wet deck.

Thank goodneth, thomeone ith coming. I flew higher to watch. Hurry up! He lookth like he might fall.

Hetty ran, feeling young again like the young, schoolgirl hockey star she had been. In her mind she could hear John's often repeated remark that, when you tackle, tackle low and push on. She dropped her shoulder, tackled low and pushed.

Thes puthed him overboard! Thave him, thave him, I thweeched but nobody heard.

John disappeared, no shout. Nothing.

"I could forgive you John, all those times when you hit me but nobody is going to hit my Bunty," shouted Hetty.

I was thocked. The woman was juth thanding there! Man over board, I thouted, man overboard! I thwooped down to show my dithpleasure in the traditional theagull manner but I mithed.

Genius

— ◆ —

There was no doubt about it Harry was a genius. He used to sit at the end of the bar drinking pint after pint and not once did I see him fall off his stool.

Now that is not why I considered him a genius after all most of those perched on the bar stools seemed to keep upright. No, Harry was special, a mathematical genius.

I'll give you an example, he sits with his back to the dartboard and as they play they don't chalk up the scores they just let Harry tot up the scores in his head. They call out, "Eighty nine, Harry takes a swig and says, "that leaves seventy seven, treble nineteen, double ten."

But that's not all. He picks winners.

He explained it to me one day. "No," he said, "I don't pick winners I calculate them. I work out their probabilities and the one with the highest probability is the winner."

I nod wisely although to be honest he loses me as soon as he starts to write in the margin of the racing news, strings of letters that, he says, represent the variables and then strings them together, adds a bit here and there and then says, "Well there you are, it's number three to win." I don't say too much. Just buy Harry another drink and take a note of his forecast.

The next day, when I get home from work I check the racing winners. There's number 3, with nice odds, winner by a nose.

I'm down the pub that evening.

Now what I haven't mentioned about Harry is that he is, how shall I put it? a bit wiffy. No that's not quite right, Harry stinks. When he gets off his stool to unload a gallon in the gents there is a blue haze around him. He does not have to worry that someone may take his stool, there's the same blue haze keeping his seat for him. To fortify myself from the eye-watering fumes, I buy myself a double Brandy and a pint for Harry.

"Here, get that down you Harry. I've been thinking about you picking winners."

"I told you, I don't pick winners. I calculate them."

A voice calls. "26" and Harry shouts back, "105 left, that's treble 17, 18 double 18."

He drinks more beer.

"Sorry Harry," I say. "You calculate winners. Do you put money on them? I mean, you could make a fortune."

"No, math's is my hobby. My pension enough for my beer and I don't need much else."

I think he could do with a good bath but I sniff my brandy and bite my tongue.

"Well Harry, perhaps you could see your way to passing on to me some of your hobby calculations."

Well, the outcome was that, for a pint, Harry would give me a number for the next day's racing when I saw him.

I put a tenner on his first tip. I mean his first calculation. It won, though the odds were a bit short. I put 50 on the next and 100 the next day. I was on easy street. I gave up my job, bought a new car, learned to spread my bets around the bookies so my winnings would go un-noticed. I made enquiries about buying a bigger house and then, Harry fell off his stool.

I was standing next to him. I thought maybe, the pints I was buying him were too much.

A voice called out, "76" From the floor Harry says, "leaves 53, that's treble 15, double 3." Then he turns his eyes to me and says, "Number 8 in the 3.30."

Harry didn't get up off the floor. Seems it was a small stroke, not the beer and he was taken to hospital.

It really shook me. I mean maybe this was Harry's last tip. I mean, calculation. I raised all the funds I could and some I couldn't and put them on number 8 and then went to visit Harry at the hospital.

I did not recognize him. Normally you can spot Harry with your eyes closed because the smell was so strong but now they had given him a bath.

He was sitting up in bed looking as good as new and smelling a lot better.

We chatted. Harry was as bright as a button. We ate the grapes I'd bought him. I thought it would be tactless to raise the subject of a new calculation for the next day and of course, I stood to make big money from number 8.

On the way out I had a word with a doctor.

"No, he'll be as good as new. Sometimes there's a little cerebral accident that seems to make little difference. Sometimes it's movement or speech and very noticeable but Mr. Saunders has no noticeable changes."

My horse lost!

Spinster

— ◆ —

"When you've finished fixing the floor, Aric, we will be about finished."

"I should hope so, it has taken all morning to fix up this tree house and I could do with a bit of relaxation."

Nida looked around with real satisfaction. Although he moaned all the time there was no doubt that Aric was a good worker.

"Oh, stop moaning Aric, it looks really lovely. The brown goes lovely with the green and when I get a bit of time to myself I am going to fix up some silk curtains to add that final touch."

Nida lay on the green and brown day bed.

"This is really comfortable." She said.

"Why don't you come over here and lay down beside me."

"Oh Nida! It's Sunday afternoon and I'm knackered. If you are expecting me to let rip with some rumpy pumpy you've worn me out already and in any case I don't hold with all this sex in the afternoons. What's wrong with our own bed, at night at home,

125

where we are not on show for everyone to see."

Nida arranged herself seductively and spoke in a honeyed sexy whisper.

"Come here you big strong boy. Lets spend a naughty Sunday afternoon making babies."

Aric's hormones gave him a surge of energy and he leapt upon the beconning Nida.

"Oh yes, that's it, you sex bomb, You do know how to hit the spot! More Aric, more."

As Aric collapsed in an orgasm she tenderly wrapped her legs around him and nuzzled the back of his neck.

"Oh, that's so good!" he murmered.

Nida smiled and bit through his neck.

Aric, convulsed in a death spasm while Nida gently disentangled her legs.

He's a bit of a runty little thing thought Nida but when the biological clock is ticking there's no time to be choosy.

I'll wrap him up in a nice bit of silk and he'll keep nice and fresh for my babies to eat.

This must be the fourth time I've finished up being a Black Widow.

It's really depressing. I think next time I'll say I'm a spinster.

All this sex and violence. It was not like this when my Mum and Dad were young. I blame it on the Tele. It's that Attenborough's fault. With his telephoto lenses, telling us innocent spiders to give him a bit more action.

Swan Song

— ◆ —

"Some enchanted evening
You may see a stranger."

"Tweet tweet, I've never heard a snail singing before. Tweet, you've got a very fine voice."

"That's very kind but I can't sing like you. I can't sing very high."

Tweet tweet, oh I'm sure you can. It's just because the air is so thick there right next to the ground. Tweet, if you were at the top of a tree you would sing like a nightingale. Tweet listen to that thrush up there on the top of that TV aerial. Tweet his voice just floats on the air."

"That's just it. I'm just a snail stuck on the ground. "

"Tweet tweet maybe I can help. Tweet I could give you a lift up and Tweet, you'll be singing like a bird."

"What lift me up with those sharp claws?"

"Tweet yes tweet. Tuck your head in your shell and I'll grip just your shell and you'll tweet be fine."

"Be careful then. Be gentle with me."

"Tweet tweet. How's that now? We're quite high. Tweet try a little song"

"Some enchanted evening' No it's no better. 'er we're getting a bit high. Where are you taking me?

"Tweet tweet I'm taking you high over that concrete pathway. Tweet tweet. You'll find the acoustics there are much better. Here we are, tweet tweet. Try your voice now."

"Some enchanted evening. No it's no bet…Ah ah ah ah

Splosh.

Lottery

——◆——

It was the Colonel's idea. He was watching the Television. Hilda, his wife, was out for the evening at some welfare committee and this gave the Colonel the opportunity ogle the voluptuous Miranda being interviewed. He, nor any hot-blooded male, was listening to what she said they were more interested in her ample bosom, long legs and bewitching face. No, thought the Colonel, forget the face just drool over that perfect body.

In truth Miranda was probably no more desirable than many other ladies but her sexual allure was fed by well-publicized stories, that Miranda enjoyed sexual activity and at a price, was available.

Miranda leaned forward, not to hear better the question but more, to display for the cameras, her expensive silicone enlargements.

"I understand er, Miranda, that you have consented to take part in the fund raising events for the relief of hunger in Africa."

She pouted her full wet lips.

"Yes, I feel I have to help all those starving children and so," she paused, "I am not just going to auction an evening with me, I am going to auction an evening and," she paused again, " An evening and how shall I put this? Well, let's just say the prize will be dinner through to breakfast."

Well, thought the Colonel, if I had the money and Hilda did not know, I 'd be there like a shot and with that thought, Hilda, the leader of the regiment returned from her committee.

The Colonel spent a restless night. His fantasy was impossible but the next best thing would be to get a, blow-by-blow, account from the winning bidder.

It was easily arranged. All unmarried, hormone rich, members of the regiment were invited to enter a raffle. The winner would use the prize to bid for the lovely Miranda and the Colonel would guarantee special leave for the lucky contestant.

Private First Class, John Taylor drew the winning ticket and the total fund ensured that it was the winning bid.

John was a shy, 18 year old, virgin and on the morning of the big day, the entire regiment was on parade to cheer off their representative and with advice ranging from underwear to a book on sexual positions, the Colonel drove John to the train station and waved John a found farewell with a tear in his eye.

Private First Class Taylor was at first, not at ease. His new underwear felt too tight and he was unused to which piece of cutlery was to be used for which dish but Miranda was at her best and he began to relax. Perhaps he drank a little too much wine. Perhaps the dozen oysters relaxed him. Perhaps Miranda's bosom hypnotized him but whatever, by the end of the meal Private John

Taylor was primed and ready for his first sexual encounter.

In the luxurious bedroom suite all inhibitions were washed away in an ample bath and his first encounter was followed by a second and third until counting and the night merged in to a blur.

Even the experienced Miranda was enchanted by the night's activities and in the morning, as John had his breakfast in bed, she asked him how he had been able to pay the money.

In a simple disarming way, John explained how the regiment had held a £2 lottery and how £10,000 had been collected and how he, a virgin, had won.

Miranda was, at heart, a kindly girl and the story flooded her with warmth.

"Look, John, I do not think it right that you should have to pay for your first experience and I think it only right that I should give you your money back. She fumbled in her purse and gave him his £2.

No Gnus

—— ◆ ——

"Ow! You're hurting me, let me go."

Grrrr, I will not. As soon as I have got my breath back I am going to kill you and eat you."

"Oh, please sir, don't kill me. I'm too young to die."

"What! Don't eat you! I am the king of the jungle and I can eat who I please."

"Please your majesty could you take you're claws off my buttocks? You're making me bleed and it's very uncomfortable."

"Do you think the king of the jungle is a fool? If I let go of you, you would be off like a flash. No in a few moments I will rip your throat out and you will not feel a thing."

"Sire, how can you be so sure that I won't feel a thing?"

"Young Antelope, I have killed more animals than you have had hot lunches and I have never had a word of complaint."

"Well you wouldn't would you, when you've finished they are all too dead to complain. Anyway, you wouldn't like me I'm too gamey."

"That, if I may say so young Antelope is nonsense. Freshly killed you will be tender and sweet, ideal for a light lunch."

"But, your Majesty, I'm not an Antelope I'm a Gnu and you won't like me."

"I have never eaten a Gnu before, so I'll be having something Gnu for lunch. There you are I have made a joke so you can die with a smile on your lips."

"Oh my god! If I hear any more Gnu jokes I'll kill myself. I've been getting them since I was Gnu born."

"I have got my breath back and there is no more time for idle chit-chat. Now, how would you like to die? I could rip your throat out but, to be honest, that way I get your blood all over my face and mane and it is the devil to clean off. I prefer to open my massive jaws, snap on to the back of your neck, one quick jerk and I am ready for a hot lunch."

"Please, please don't kill me. I'm too young to die. I haven't even got all my hormones yet. Next Spring would be my first rutting season and I was really looking forward to spreading myself about a bit and finding out the meaning of life and have you no pity? I am an orphan."

"You mean you have no father or mother?"

"Well your majesty, we Gnus have a saying; It's a wise Gnu that

Gnu his own father, and my mother was shot by bush meat poachers not long after I was born."

"Aha! Now we're getting to the truth, the poachers would not have killed your mother if Gnus were not good to eat. So let me be at you."

"No no Sire! Gnus are only good to eat if they are grilled very slowly over a hot fire. Then they are delicious but Sire, your majesty, you mean to eat me raw and as I have said, Gamey. Why not let me fix you a nice grass sandwich."

"No, I am ready for my lunch now. How do you want to be killed? A quick snap of the neck or your throat ripped out."

"Well, your majesty, if I am to die I think I would wish to face my death bravely so I must meet my death face to face."

"Grrr, right then let me get at your throat. Grrr; I say Gnu old chap, would you mind closing your eyes. I do not like those big brown eyes staring at me while I kill you."

"Would it help your majesty if I were to explain that I am an illegal immigrant on this game reserve and I smuggled myself here to avoid death from the poachers and as you are king of the forest I believe correct procedure is that I apply to you for asylum."

"Grrr, why did you not tell me that in the first place? Now you have put me off my lunch. Very well, using my royal prerogative I grant you permission to stay here. Now hop off before I change my mind."

"Little Anty, where have you been I've been looking for you everywhere.

"Sorry Mumsey, I've been talking to that lion over there. He's rather stupid but I think we'd better move away in case he hears you call me Anty."

Pulling Power

— ◆ —

George viewed his face in the mirror. Not bad, well perhaps, not good! He was not bad looking it was just that he was not good looking. He was not tall but then, he was not short. He was just, ordinary. Before his Mum had died she was always telling him he should get a nice girl friend and settle down but none of the few girls he had met seemed at all interested in George.

Except Elizabeth Fossey who had lived in Croscombe just a couple of miles away. His heart gave a little skip as he thought of Elizabeth. She had been 16 and he 17. Each day, after school in Wells they would walk home across the fields, sometimes just talking, sometimes holding hands and just sometimes exchanging a light kiss. He had left school at 18 to work with his father on their small farm at Dinder. Elizabeth Fossey, had achieved good A levels and had gone away to university.

The Fossey family had moved away from Croscombe breaking, for George, any hope of contact with their daughter. George, with his parents both dead scraped a lonely existence on the small farm. Sometimes, he would attend the Young Farmers parties in Wells but each time George would make the return journey, across the meadows alone.

Most evenings when it was too dark for more work, George would watch Television. He watched adverts where young men sprayed under-arm deodorant or after-shave and hoards of nubile young ladies would hurl themselves at them. Hope springs eternal and George's bathroom was stuffed with sprays, roll-ons and lotions but no lovely maiden ever lusted after George.

September brought clear skies a perfect harvest and glorious sunsets but George's heart was not lifted. Next Saturday was the Young Farmers' Harvest Home Ball and he would go and knew he would return alone. As he walked he gloomily surveyed his hedges and ditches. They would be his next task. There, in the hedge, he saw the bright red spur of an Arum Lily and he remembered the other names; Cuckoo Pintle or Parson's Pintle because of the phallic shape. He remembered the folklore, which suggested the pulling power of the pintle and thought well it can't do worse than all those sprays I've wasted my money on.

On the evening of the Ball George, did not stint the expensive smellies but before he put his newly cleaned shoes on he placed in the right shoe a pintle saying; "I place you in my shoe, let all girls be drawn to you."

For George, the ball was a disaster. He was a wallflower and as the evening wore on, he was a tipsy wallflower. He blundered his way home along the path across the meadows and collapsed in a drunken heap on his lonely bed.

He awoke early Sunday morning. He was still wearing his good suit and his right shoe remained on his foot. His head hurt. His foot hurt. He kicked off his shoe and it seemed that, released from pressure, the foot swelled. He had a hot bath and soaked his foot.

His head felt better but his foot throbbed. The pain increased. He checked the local paper to find out which Chemist had the Sunday emergency service. Boots in Hope Street, 10 to 11.

He could not get a shoe on and had to cut away part of the toe of his old trainers to get something on his foot. The clutch and brake pedals in his old car sent sharp pains running up his leg but he drove the few miles to Wells carefully and slowly.

Hope Street echoed to the church bells as George eased himself out of the car and hobbled in to Boots.

"The store was empty, just one assistant at the far counter.

"Look I'm sorry to be such a bother but I seem to have got a very painful foot and I wondered if your pharmacist might suggest something to help."

"I'll find out if she will look at it for you if you will sit over there." She disappeared into the pharmacy and he could just see two heads peering at him through the glass partition. He bent to loosen his trainer and first saw, trim brown shoes, a white coat and heard a voice saying,

"Hullo George."

Elizabeth Fossey, relief Pharmacist, smiled at her first and only love and her heart skipped a beat. George leapt to his feet. His foot ceased to hurt and his heart skipped a beat.

Home From Home

——— ◆ ———

Have you ever been stuck on a country lane behind a towed caravan? It is so frustrating, you want to move on but you move just at a snails pace.

Well if you think it's bad, spare a thought for the poor chap ahead who is trying his best to make time but is doomed to drag around his mobile home. Well that's just like me.

Perhaps I should introduce myself. My name is Perry Winkle. It's a stupid name I know but when I was born my Mum thought I was just like a flower. She said my eyes were like blue periwinkles. It's stupid really, I mean I'm not a flower and I'm not a winkle, which brings me back to where I started. Like the man with a caravan I'm stuck with my home. All my life I have wanted to leave home but I can't. I am a snail; born with the wanderlust to just get up and leave home.

I want to feel the wind in my hair. I'd like to be a cowboy racing on my fiery mustang across a wide-open prairie.

But just because I've always got this home stuck on my back does not mean I can't travel the world. For example, I once stowed away in a lorry load of topsoil and found myself being spread on the lawns at the tower of London. It was all very exciting but I soon realized that those Ravens have got dangerous beaks and given half a chance they would have had me for breakfast. So, as quick as I could I hurried to the nearest door and found myself in the white tower. I was stuck there for two days. Of course the crown jewels were all very interesting but you can't eat them. I escaped on the bottom of a backpack carried by an Australian tourist.

I don't think snails are designed for air travel but I made it to Melbourne.

For a while I quite liked Australia. The local snails spoke with a peculiar accent but they all treated me with respect as it was widely assumed that I must be the most traveled snail in the whole of snail history.

I met and married a nice Aussie snail called Fair Dinkum and we had loads of babies. I should have been content but as time passed I realized that the old wanderlust was still in me and strangely telling me it was time to go back to my home country.

I said a fond farewell to Fair Dinkum and the kids and set off.

I hitched a ride in a crate of Anchor Butter. It was freezing and I was lucky to be able to pull right back in to my shell, close the lid and snooze away the time.

I made it back to a shelf in the CO-OP in my hometown of Frinton From there, hanging on to a slow moving Zimmer Frame I moved to the Community center and that's where you find me now.

Does anybody here have a nice garden and would be pleased to accommodate a well traveled snail who wants to settle down and tell tall stories about his travels.

Ambition

— ◆ —

When I was young my mum said I had beautiful teeth and that I should smile more often but I don't think a smile looks right when you are an alligator. I mean, when I flash my teeth it's supposed to scare the living daylights out of you.

I was born in Florida and had a very happy childhood. Most days I would lie, with my brothers and sisters on the banks of the river and soak up the sun. Mum was very concerned that we did not get sunburn and made sure those generous layers of, factor 25, river mud, protected us.

When we were hungry we would just float in the water looking like logs and catch some unwary tidbit that came to have a drink. For us, the Florida water glades were paradise.

It was my ambition that ruined it for me. I remember saying to my brother Arnold, "Don't you ever think that there's more to life than lazing in the sun getting a tan. Don't you think we should be making something of ourselves"

"Nop!"

Arnold is a 'Gaitor of few words.

But I wanted to get on, become chief 'Gaitor or something, see the world, make something of myself.

So I left home, swam up stream, towards civilization.

I had never seen Americans before. Lots of them live in very grand residences, close by the waters edge of the bayous. I spent weeks just watching the silly things they did.

There were paths at the water's edge and every morning there were endless streams of joggers, dog walkers, skaters, skate boarders, cyclists, eaters and drinkers. Some combined several activities at the same time. For example, many joggers had dogs, held in one hand and a high-energy drink to replace at once those calories that jogging had used. Many walkers would graze on burgers as they conducted their morning rituals.

I too got a taste for fast food so that, for several weeks, I scavenged the quiet banks eating discarded burgers. I loved the mayo' and pickles.

There is, I think, some devil in my nature that pushes me to do something I shouldn't do and I developed a fascination for a little dog that was proudly paraded along the path every day. It wore a rosette on its collar and from the conversations I overheard, I had learned that this small walking wig had won some competition at Crufts, over the water.

Each day I lay in the water, looking like a log, watching the dog's very effeminate owner, parade up and down. He held a short lead out high so that the poor dog had to hold its head up or else be strangled.

144

I knew it would not be good for me. I knew it would probably give me a hairball but I could not resist the impulse. I floated nearer and as it passed by I leaped up the bank, flashed my beautiful teeth and caught it.

I was back in the water like a flash but the stupid owner was still holding the lead and I pulled him in.

The owner was thrashing about in the water screaming and somebody from one of the house came running out with a huge shotgun and shot me. I wish I could say that I eat a hearty breakfast before I died but I was right, the damned dog was just a mass of tasteless hair with not enough meat to make a good burger.

The shotgun pellets made a mess of a lot of my skin but after tanning, there was enough of me to make a Versace handbag with matching knee length boots. Some days I am proudly paraded along the water's edge. I get my own back when I can. I hide her car keys in the lining when it's raining so that she gets soaked looking for them to unlock her car and I'm working on her bunions.

Cliff Hangar

— ◆ —

"A trumpet shall sound," Maestro looks at me and I stand up. Flick the valves, lick my lips and I'm ready, I hope.

I should not be here really but Fulford rang this morning to say that he had cut his lip shaving and would not be able to play. It's a poor excuse really. All the orchestra knows that the poor little wimp gets regularly beaten by his dominating wife and that it was only a matter of time before she fetched him one round the lip. But, what's a fat lip for Fulford is good luck for me. I'm a good trumpet player but I was Silver Band trained rather than a product of academic musical training like the rest and I feel inferior.

Anyway! Maestro called me in this morning and asked me if I was able to play trumpet solo at tonight's performance so here I am, Westminster Abbey, top row standing. Maestro said I should stand so that the audience should experience what was in effect a duet of solo tenor and Trumpet.

He is a super tenor, tubby with a little moustache; I think the soprano has got the hots for him she's looking up at him as though she wants to eat him.

Of course I told Maestro that I was up for it. What I did not tell him was the dream I had last night. How I was standing alone on stage, with a large crowd looking on. I raise my trumpet to my lips, hit the note and, nothing. Well not exactly nothing, no sound just large bubble from the bell. The audience is laughing. I blow again and a huge bubble appears. My trousers seem to be slipping down and the audience is throwing rotten fruit.

Angela is sitting in the front row. She is sneering. I just pray that my dream is not prophetic. My pulse is raising, Maestro looks at me ready to give me the beat.

Angela is sitting just below me. She plays first cello. I have never met anyone like her. She is beautiful, educated, intelligent and she holds that Cello between her knees like she was making love to it. I hope that my performance this evening will impress her and maybe we would make music together without the aid of any musical instruments. I can imagine Angela, holding me like the Cello with her hands clutched round my back. A man could die happy between Angela's knees.

But, what if my dream becomes reality. I remember going to a concert where a flutist was giving a recital and instead of a pure first note he got a gob of spit on the mouthpiece and all he got was a gurgle. I give him full marks for bravery. He stopped, got out a handkerchief, wiped the mouthpiece and started again but I blushed for him all the way through the recital.

My God! It could happen to me.

Angela looks up. She is smiling at me. Is that a promise of pleasures to come?

Sweat is pouring down both sides of my face. I taste the salt on my lips. Have I time to wipe my mouth? No, now is the moment.

It is the Easter concert at Westminster Abbey, the Messiah and I John Brown, brass band player from Pickerskill, new member of the BBC Symphony Orchestra am about to make an absolute idiot of myself.

Maestro twitches a nonchalant baton at me and I hit the note.

It is as though my horn is made of pure gold. The liquid notes caress every nook and cranny of the Abbey.

"And the dead shall be raised."

My bit again, I hope Angela finds my golden horn irresistible.

Printed in the United Kingdom
by Lightning Source UK Ltd.
129338UK00001B/316-321/P